FORMER BASEBALL PLAYER SUCKS AT CROWDFUNDING

A TIME TRAVEL ADVENTURE

By Dan Ryckert

This book is purely a work of fiction. Any similarities to actual events or people is purely coincidental. Former Baseball Player is in no way meant to represent any actual former athlete of any description.

©2013 Up To Something Publishing

FORMER BASEBALL PLAYER SUCKS AT CROWDFUNDING

Chapter One

By Dan Ryckert

The Year 2013

As he pulled out of the liquor store parking lot, renowned author Dan Ryckert heard a rumble in the seat next to him. Glancing at his iPhone, he saw that the incoming text was from his boss. Assuming it was work-related, the consummate professional immediately checked to see if there were pressing matters that needed attention.

"Former Baseball Player's crowdfunded podcast has pulled in $20," it read.

"Bahahahahahahaha," responded the author of *Air Force Gator* and *Air Force Gator 2: Scales of Justice*, two successful novels that feature fantastic average review scores on leading online retailers.

His knee-jerk reaction of laughter quickly turned into an idea.

"I bet I could raise more than that for absolutely nothing," he thought.

Ryckert laughed to himself at the idea of raising money for no reason at all as he drove to his friend's house for a night of watching Wrestlemania VII. There, he drank from his 40-ounce bottle of delicious and affordable Mickey's malt liquor as he watched The Undertaker piledrive Superfly Jimmy Snuka, Macho Man

Randy Savage reunite with the lovely Miss Elizabeth, and Regis Philbin get kinda racist when he interviewed those Japanese guys. Watching wrestling was always an enjoyable affair for the handsome 29 year-old, but he couldn't shake the silly idea that had been bouncing around his head from before.

"No, seriously," he thought. "People would totally give me money if I started some dumbass crowdfunder to make fun of that dipshit."

For years, Former Baseball Player had demonstrated a remarkable lack of self-awareness and an equally astounding lack of intelligence. Throughout the course of his life, the only area in which Former Baseball Player found a modicum of success was professional baseball.

He began playing as a child in the Pacific Northwest, which is very far away from Cuba. Despite impressing his elementary school classmates with his seemingly natural ability, he found it harder and harder to get by as the years progressed. As a college student, he began recreationally experimenting with illegal drugs. At first, these were relegated to back alley drug deals in a desperate effort to enlarge his woefully tiny penis. Things soon escalated, as Former Baseball Player saw the possibilities in performance-enhancing drugs.

Steroids were a shortcut to the fame and fortune that Former Baseball Player craved in an effort to compensate for his almost invisible

FORMER BASEBALL PLAYER SUCKS AT CROWDFUNDING

penis. Many nights in college and beyond were spent bent over a sink, crying as he injected needle after needle into his buttocks.

"Someday they'll like me," Former Baseball Player would say through tears. "Someday I'll be big and strong and rich and I'll have a human-sized penis. And then, I can ask all my fans to give me money for a radio show and it'll totally work."

After years and years of pumping his body full of illegal drugs, he found the attention he craved in a decade-plus baseball career. These boring years ended, and he quickly saw his moment in the sun slipping through his fingers.

"They don't care anymore," Former Baseball Player found himself thinking each and every day. "And my dick is still so small and no lady will ever touch it. Sometimes I wonder why I'm even here anymore."

His anger lingered for years until one lonely night, Former Baseball Player had a booze-fueled vision.

"I know! I'll rat out all my friends and make millions!"

Outside of artificially enhancing his body to succeed at sports, the only ability Former Baseball Player possessed was being a total turd to everyone around him. Utilizing this natural ability to the fullest, he wrote a big dumb book that made everyone hate him and got his former teammates into a lot of trouble.

Millions were made off this book, but Former Baseball Player was quick to waste it all on stupid shirts, Hummers, tanning booths, fat prostitutes, and desperate attempts to increase his penis size via black market medications and appointments with shady doctors. By 2013, he was flat broke.

With neither the attention he once received or the money he earned in such a shitty fashion, his anguish returned. Night after night, he cried in front of a computer screen while watching pornography that he was stupid enough to pay for. After fruitlessly attempting to pleasure himself with his non-functioning and small penis, he gave up and turned to social media in a plea for attention.

"got lotsa good ideas but need 2 be herd. id be president if u all could hear the stuf in my brain," read his post. Thousands of people followed him on social media out of morbid curiosity, curious to hear what would come out of his dipshit mouth next. That fateful night, one of his followers responded.

"Just start a crowdfunding campaign, dumbass," read the response.

Former Baseball Player asked his agent what that meant, and within days, his campaign was born. Since he had never heard of a podcast, the dipshit attempted to raise $15,000 for equipment to start his own terrestrial radio program. Despite attempting to leverage his social media notoriety for a quick buck, he had only raised twenty measly dollars in 24 hours.

FORMER BASEBALL PLAYER SUCKS AT CROWDFUNDING

Halfway across the country, Dan Ryckert prepared his rival campaign.

"Trust me, guys," Ryckert said to his friends as they watched WrestleMania. "No one wants that butthole to have his own radio show, so he won't raise shit."

"Yeah," replied Ryckert's friend. "But why would anyone give you money for nothing?"

"Because it's funny! I'm some gaming journalist with a fraction of his followers, but people will give me money just to help me mock that dipshit. Trust me on this one."

Ryckert was met with skepticism, but knew that he'd win his battle with Former Baseball Player. He drove home, grabbed a couple more Mickey's, and spent an hour preparing his campaign with descriptions of its useless nature. He promised nothing of value, saying that if funded, the campaign would result in something that was technically a book that someone could buy. After making a header image with his fantastic photo editing skills, the campaign was ready to go.

Within hours of the campaign going live, Ryckert destroyed Former Baseball Player's tally tenfold. The talented and humorous Jeff Gerstmann was first to chip in, followed by the Diet Coke-drinking weirdo John Drake. Minutes later, Dan Ryckert's ambitious, supportive, and loving mother Terri Hannam backed the campaign and even sent him a pretty sweet Crock Pot from Amazon. Next up was Zachary Snader, a nice dude that Ryckert met at a party in LA earlier in the year. Dan didn't know Chris Denahy, but this backer sounded pretty cool since he claims to have once used the toilet of the Prime Minister of Australia.

For the next several days, awesome followers of Dan Ryckert used their wallets to show their support of the campaign and take part in the public mockery of Former Baseball Player. Thousands of dollars came in to Ryckert's while Former Baseball Player struggled to hit three digits. When the dust settled, it was clear that Dan Ryckert was superior to Former Baseball Player in every way.

Back in the Pacific Northwest, Former Baseball Player had spent the last month feverishly refreshing his crowdfunding page to no avail. No one cared about his stupid thing, because they already got their fill of his dumbass thoughts on social media channels.

"Why did this guy make so much more than me?" Former Baseball Player said to himself as he looked at Ryckert's campaign. "This sucks. I want some of that money."

After spending a week trying to figure out how to use the internet to book plane tickets, he gave up and had his manager book him tickets to Minnesota. Packing his bag full of protein supplements and titty magazines, Former Baseball Player and his big fat head were on their way to the upper Midwest.

Landing at the airport, he forgot to grab his bags before departing for downtown because he's stupid. He wandered around the large

FORMER BASEBALL PLAYER SUCKS AT CROWDFUNDING

airport for six hours before finding his way to the light rail, but he managed to stumble on and begin heading in the general direction of downtown Minneapolis.

Several stops away from downtown, a light rail officer approached Former Baseball Player.

"Can I see your ticket please?"

"Wha?" Former Baseball Player responded, a string of drool escaping from his mouth.

"Get off the train, dummy."

Kicked off the light rail, Former Baseball Player spent the next two days wandering the streets of Minneapolis searching for Ryckert's location. A basic internet search would have made this much simpler for the meathead, but he instead spent hours talking to confused bus drivers, unsuccessfully mugging children, and eating unfinished chicken wings that he found in public dumpsters.

Tired, hungry, and confused, he had almost given up hope when he spotted a sign that read "PRO WRESTLING TONIGHT." Knowing that Ryckert was a longtime fan of sports entertainment, he camped out near the front door of the bar and waited for the show to end. An hour later, Ryckert emerged with friends.

"Dan Ryckert!" Former Baseball Player yelled.

Ryckert turned, and a look of shock immediately spread across his face.

"Holy shit," Ryckert said to his friends. "It's Former Baseball Player. Guys, I'll meet you at the bar later. I gotta go see what this is all about."

As Ryckert approached Former Baseball Player, he quickly noticed how dirty, leathery, and weird he looked in person.

"This is super weird," Ryckert said. "What are you doing here in Minneapolis?"

"Gimme some money."

"What? No. I don't have much."

"But you made so much more than me," Former Baseball Player said. "Can I have it?"

"No way. This is gonna help me pay for rent, get me to WrestleMania XXX, and cover the costs of putting together a new book that has nothing to do with you or any real-life individuals. Plus, I gotta pay to send out all those signed copies of *Air Force Gator* and *Air Force Gator 2: Scales of Justice* to my followers, who are easily the greatest followers in the world."

"Shut up," Former Baseball Player said. "I want money."

"You were a super-rich millionaire," Ryckert said. "Can't you pay for your own radio show?"

"Naw, I spent it all on Corn Nuts and fat prostitutes."

"Well that's stupid, Former Baseball Player. You can't expect me to give you a handout just because you were irresponsible and dumb."

FORMER BASEBALL PLAYER SUCKS AT CROWDFUNDING

Former Baseball Player reached for Ryckert's pocket, attempting to grab his wallet before the author pulled back.

"You can't go through life being an asshole to everyone you meet, and then just expect people to give you money," Ryckert said. "The only reason you had money in the first place is because you cheated in sports and then threw all your friends under the bus. Now you've wasted it all, and you want hard-working people to give you more money? That's insane."

"Well fuck you!," Former Baseball Player said as he began crying. He punched Ryckert in the testicles, then ran away sobbing as the author slumped to the sidewalk.

"Fuck you, Former Baseball Player!" Ryckert yelled down the street as he shook his fist. "You'll get what's coming to you!"

Former Baseball Player ran for a quarter of a mile before he got tired, as it had been hours since his last massive injection of steroids. Finding himself on the Hennepin Bridge, he looked out at the water of the Mississippi River. Countless memories of his past ran through his head. That time he knocked groceries out of that lady's hands for no reason. That time he threw firecrackers over the fence into an elementary school's recess. That time he tried to hit Bon Jovi with a pie during a benefit concert. That time he was banned from Arsenio Hall for giving the host a wedgie.

"Shit," Former Baseball Player said. "Maybe I really do suck."

He stepped over the railing of the bridge and stared at the water below. Despite not having much working knowledge of human anatomy, he was somewhat sure that he wouldn't be able to breathe underwater.

"Goodbye, world. You're about to be short one asshole."

Stepping off the concrete, he felt his stomach rise inside of him as his body began to plummet. A dopey yell escaped from his lips as he felt the cold air rush towards him and saw the river rising from below.

Suddenly, a bright purple light appeared above the water. A shifting, colorful portal opened out of nowhere, and Former Baseball Player braced himself for impact as his body entered the mysterious wormhole.

FORMER BASEBALL PLAYER SUCKS AT CROWDFUNDING

Chapter Two

By Justin McElroy (@JustinMcElroy)

The Year 503

It all came down to instinct.
Former Baseball Players never lose it, though it may dull over time, it's never really gone. If something is flying through the air, they catch it. It's all they know.
So when Former Baseball Player tumbled out of the portal and saw glistening metal hurtling through the air, he didn't think. He doesn't think. He can't think. He catches it.
"Zounds!" a voice called out, "that was intended for me!"
Former Baseball Player turned and looked the source of the voice over, from his metal arms and legs to his shiny metal face. Sure, the man tried to cover up with a dumb cape with a lion on it, but FBP saw right through the disguise.
"Sorry, robot, but I'm keeping your sword. Better luck next time."
FBP casually threw the sword over his shoulder, opening up a gash about an inch deep, because the sword was very sharp. He almost cried out, but he wasn't about to give the robot the satisfaction of being all smug about his metal skin.

"MORTAL!" a voice quaked from beneath the surface of the nearby lake as a naked woman slowly emerged from its surface.

Former Baseball Player was frozen in place as her beauty washed over him. His mind raced as he tried to find the words that could properly encapsulate the impeccable creature that now hovered inches above the rippling surface of the water.

"I LIKE YOUR JUGS!" he called out, giving her a thumbs up. He had nailed it.

"MORTAL!" she called again, even more furious. A pulsating red aura emanated from her skin as she fumed. "You hold in your hand Excalibur, an ancient blade of unimaginable power. It was not intended for the likes of you. That blade must be returned to Arthur, a good and noble leader who shall lead this land to safety and prosperity."

"Arthur?" Former Baseball Player shot a dirty look to Excalibur's intended recipient. "You mean the robot? Why does a robot need a sword? Doesn't he have laser eyes or..."

"I'm not a robot you imbecile," Arthur struggled towards Former Baseball Player, his armor sinking with each step into the muddy bank of the lake. "I don't even know the word."

"Robot, don't try to bullshit me, I used to play baseball. You have metal skin, you walk funny, you're a robot." Former Baseball Player smiled, so rarely had his attempts to use logic panned out so well. "Does Arthur stand for something? Like Awesome Robot ... That Has..."

FORMER BASEBALL PLAYER SUCKS AT CROWDFUNDING

"BUFFOON!" Arthur screamed, finally at the side of the oddly-muscled interloper.

"Thanks for the help robot, but I need an 'I' word next," said FBP as he stroked his dinner roll-shaped chin. "Or is it an 'E'?"

"I am wearing armor, you cretin!" Arthur flipped up his helmet. "Do you see? I am a Child of God, just as yourself!"

"Arthur speaks true," the Lady of the Lake called out, her temper softening. She had heard rumors of women who had become smitten with ogres, giving over their bodies in exchange for promises of eternal devotion and protection from the countless dangers that roamed the countryside.

This strange visitor had such an oddly shaped head and the intellect of a distracted toddler. Clearly he was the product of one of these ghastly unions.

"He wears armor because he is a knight," she cooed as she would to a misbehaving puppy. "A brave warrior who will someday be king."

"Hell, I could be king," FBP scoffed. "I once ran for mayor of Quebec, but they disqualified me just because I'm not from Canada."

"Don't you mean Toronto?" Arthur asked under his breath.

"No, robot, I mean Quebec. Definitely not Toronto. Quebec. What kind of idiot would run for mayor of Toronto if he's not Canadian? Whatever...I'm the king now." Former Baseball Player struggled to maintain consciousness as blood gushed from his shoulder. "I've got the sword and you can make me robot skin. Just be sure to make the crotch part really small on account of my penis is very tiny."

FBP peered at the lake babe to see if that raised an eyebrow, but her expression was unchanged, she remained furious and damp.

Nice. She was into it.

He was moments away from explaining the subtle pleasures of making love to a tiny-penised man when heard the first scream echo from over the hill.

"Arthur! Arthur where art thou!?"

The screams were punctuated by clanks as a knight tromped down the hillside. Each step seemed a struggle, his armor was drenched in blood that had already begun to dry in the Avalon sun.

He collapsed, rolling the final few feet down the hill. Arthur awkwardly clanked to his side.

"Ye gods, Sir Bedivere! What has happened, what has befallen thee?"

Bedivere flipped up the conical visor of his hounskull. It wasn't until then that Former Baseball Player noticed that the spot where Bedivere's left hand should be had been replaced by a ragged, bloody stump.

"It's ... it's the Saxons, m'lord. They've ... they've taken Camelot."

The two horses sped across the fields as Former Baseball Player and Arthur desperately tried to close the miles between them and Arthur's castle.

"I'm sorry your friend died, but I'm glad I could put his horse to use," FBP smacked Arthur on one metal-clad shoulder speaking gingerly, even though he knew robots didn't have feelings really. "I think he would have wanted it this way."

"I'm not so sure." Arthur glared straight ahead, afraid he'd be unable to keep himself from a mortal sin if he looked into FBP's doughy face.

"No? You don't think he would be proud that his horse is being ridden by King Baseball?"

"I doubt it very much, in fact. I think I began to suspect it when he yelled 'Please, don't take my horse, I'm still alive and would like very much to ride back to safety at some point.'"

FBP faked a confused look, which wasn't tough, as it was basically his default expression. "I...didn't hear that. Maybe he was just joking?"

"Mayhaps," said Arthur, slicing into the horizon with his glare. "But when he continued 'I know you can hear me, you're three feet away from me. This is not a joke, I'm not joking, I'll die without medical attenti..'"

The breath he needed to finish his sentence was suddenly stolen by the sight of his home being slowly dismantled by twisting spires of flame.

"Sweet...merciful...lord!"

Former Baseball Player turned to Arthur, annoyed. "Yeah? What do you want?"

Arthur wept.

He allowed himself just a moment of despair before storming into the battle, his sword aloft. (Well, technically *his* sword was in the fleshy mitt of the halfling riding at his side, but he luckily carried a spare.)

An instant before he could call for his men and rally them to his side, a Saxxon's club thudded into the stomach of his mail. He clattered to the ground, gasping for breath that would not come. Former Baseball Player turned towards the horrific clang.

The Saxxon had gotten a cheap shot in and FBP didn't like it one bit especially considering A.R.T.H.I.R.'s various servos and widgets didn't seem to be powerful enough to lift him off the ground.

The Saxxon smacked the thick club against his shield, taunting his engorged opponent as he smiled through his beard with a mouth that was more rot than teeth. His eyes dared Former Baseball Player to take his shot.

Tensing all of his favorite muscles, FBP swung Excalibur with a wide grin. Its perfectly honed blade whistled towards the Saxxon's throat ... and then missed it entirely.

"Piece of shit! Fuck swords!" FBP threw the sacred weapon to the ground and farted on it for good measure. He just wasn't a swordsman, and he had to make his peace with that.

FORMER BASEBALL PLAYER SUCKS AT CROWDFUNDING

He had just a moment to reflect on this truism before he spotted a dozen more Saxxon's roaring to their comrade's side.

He was fucked.

A breeze not an inch from his ear and a wet thud spun him around to see the first Saxxon fall to his knees, a faucet of blood gushing out of Arthur's crossbow bolt now buried in his heart. FBP made a mental note to congratulate his robot buddy on the shot after the battle.

The Saxxon's club rolled from his limp hand as FBP somersaulted towards it. At least, he had *intended* to somersault. What resulted was really more of a stumble into the mud and a brief crawl, but it got the job done.

He scooped the narrow end into his hand and reared its heft above his still-seeping shoulder wound. He may not have known dick about swords, but if there was one thing he could handle it was whacking stuff with a heavy stick.

"WOOSH!" was not the sound the club made as it swung toward the dozen Saxxons that leapt towards him but the sound that Former Baseball Player made with his mouth as his swung, attempting to heighten the drama.

His rippling arm shook as the makeshift bat connected with the head of the first Saxxon. A warm jet of blood shot from his head and FBP had to duck to avoid the path of the eyeball he had just dislodged.

A second Saxxon with wild shocks of red hair and the slightest hint of fear in his eyes started for FBP.

"Go ahead," FBP grimaced. "Make my day. Also, tell everybody I said that first, OK? Remember that I said that about making my day."

None of the Saxxons reached for paper or anything, so he really hoped the ginger Saxxon would remember. Though that became exponentially less likely as FBP turned the thug's brains into baseball bat jelly.

Dozens of swings and liters of Saxxon blood later, Former Baseball Player finally turned away from his grim work to see that A.R.T.H.I.R. and his robot buddies were watching him with a sort of fascinated horror, their mouths agape.

"You...you killed all of them!" said Sir Gareth.

"You didn't leave any for us!" Sir Percivale complained.

"You [gasp] you stole my [gasp] horse!" Bedivere wheezed.

"OK, OK, I get it," Former Baseball Player put his hands up as he attempted mock humility. "You want autographs, no problem. Who has a Sharpie?"

All the knights raised the tips of their swords aloft.

"No, not a sword, I mean...ugh, forget it," FBP dipped his finger into a puddle of Saxxon blood and smeared his initials into the tunic of a protesting Sir Percivale. He realized too late he had made the "B" backwards, but he doubted these guys could read anyway. "Stay in school and stuff."

"You moron!" Arthur pushed his way to the front of the group.

"Hey, how dare you address King Baseball that way?"

"You dropped the sword, I'm king again," Arthur dangled Excalibur in front of FBP's still-blood-crazed eyes.

"God dammit, you are one sneaky robot."

"Yes, I am. I am also your king and as such, I demand to know..." Arthur leaned in conspiratorially, "...what is the secret of your great strength? I have never seen a man or half-man fight with such power."

FBP could smell a trap when he...smelled one. "Oh, you know. Just like, plenty of water and...ummm, sunlight and...you know."

Arthur eyed the burly liar suspiciously. "And that's it?"

"OK, well," FBP couldn't resist. "My power is largely taken from — well, I guess you'd call it a magic potion that makes your muscles really big. Yeah, it's a potion. That's it."

"Astounding!" cried a curdled voice from the rear of the crowd. Merlin pushed his way to Arthur's side. "Could you replicate this potion for us, Mister Ogre? The next wave of Saxxons will be upon us any moment and we must do something to turn the tide or risk losing Camelot forever!"

FBP scoffed, his arms crossed. "First, I'm not an ogre, I'm Cuban. NO, wait, I'm from the Pacific Northwest. Not Cuban. Second...just show me to your science shit, Gandalf."

With the laser-like focus of a cardiovascular surgeon, Former Baseball Player dripped the last bit of purple goo into the vial, joining the rust-colored liquid it was already half full with.

He took a step back, his hands above his head.

"There, I did it. I made steroids."

Merlin cautiously joined his side, suspiciously eyeing the vial, still fully expecting an explosion.

"Stare-oids? What manner of magicks are they?"

FBP laughed in the old man's face, droplets of half-ogre spittle flecking into his beard. "It's not magic, you dumb old dude, it's science. Sci-ence. Like microscopes and germs and the sun. You know...science."

Merlin, not wanting to be the butt of more of FBP's jokes, nodded thoughtfully.

Throughout the journey to Merlin's tower, Former Baseball Player had mocked Merlin incessantly, with venom-tipped barbs like "Nice robes, Doctor Gay" and "Your old beard smells like a fart." Merlin had faked serenity, but too many flashbacks to being called Doctor Gay during his Hogwarts days had shaken him badly.

FORMER BASEBALL PLAYER SUCKS AT CROWDFUNDING

"Will you try it?" the old wizard asked tentatively, trying to ignore the smell of his own beard.

"Oh no, I can't do that, see, it's already made me really strong so like, if I took more, I'd just be way too strong, like God or something."

"I see," Merlin entwined his fingers, keeping them in front of himself like a man at prayer. "In that case, I will call for Sir Gaheris!"

A few minutes later, Sir Gaheris ducked his head nervously into Merlin's room. A spindly man with arms like sun-warmed Laffy Taffy, everyone knew that — despite his kind heart and bravery — he only had a seat at the round table because Arthur was his uncle.

Merlin waved him impatiently into the room. "Yes Gaheris, come in, come in."

Gaheris, in his tunic that was two sizes too big for his diminutive frame, hobbled to the center of the cobblestone floor, Arthur in tow. The contrast between Arthur's linebacker's frame and Gaheris' wispy question mark of a silhouette made the nephew look even more pitiful.

"You're sure about this, interloper?" Arthur spat, his arms folded resolutely in front of him.

"Listen, ARTHIR," FBP put a hand on the king's armored shoulder. "I know you're not programmed to believe in stuff, but this is *science*. You should love science, you wouldn't be here without science."

Arthur shrugged the meaty paw from his armor. "Fine, as you say. We are desperate and are left with no other possible way to defend ourselves from the Saxxon onslaught."

"M'lord," Merlin scuffed to a drapery against one wall of the room hiding a seven-foot-tall circular shape. "I have taken precautions, should the potion turn Gaheris into a demon or ogre like our friend here."

"Hey!" FBP strode towards Merlin to give him a punch right in his weird beard, but was halted by what Merlin revealed with a tug on the ratty fabric.

At first it was just a simple golden hoop, but as light from the afternoon sun struck it, it began to pulse with a sort of shimmer that ran the length of the circle like a ball in a roulette wheel. As it picked up momentum, the age-worn granite behind the hoop appeared to suck in, as though it was nothing more than tissue being pulled from the other side of the wall.

The men, all but Merlin, stared with mouths agape. The wizard broke the stunned silence.

"We have no idea where the portal leads, m'lord, but it will at least banish Gaheris from the room should he prove to be … uncooperative."

Arthur placed his hands on Gaheris' diminutive shoulders, though not fully resting them there so as not to shatter his nephew's fragile shoulder blades with the weight of his gauntlets.

FORMER BASEBALL PLAYER SUCKS AT CROWDFUNDING

"My boy, you know you don't *have* to do this, aye?" Arthur's eyes glistened with a mix of fear and pride.

Gaheris nodded.

"Yes, my liege. But this is not just my duty, it's the only way I may be of service to the kingdom, heaven knows I've never contributed before."

"Nonsense! You tend..."

"*Other* than tending to the chickens, uncle."

The two shared a solemn hug until FBP broke the moment.

"So, umm, you basically just want to, you know, drink this and you'll get just really strong. Like me."

Gaheris reached for the vial, his fingers looking more like an octogenarian's in the shadow of FBP's turkey sausage digits. He took one long breath and upended the vial, his eyes wide with anticipatory panic.

There was nothing.

Then Gaheris coughed once.

And died.

Former Baseball Player thought this might happen. He wasn't sure why he had assumed he'd be able to replicate the formula for steroids based solely on instinct, but he knew there was a chance, however slim, he wouldn't nail it on the first try.

"I shoulda added more of the green stuff, I think," he sighed, returning to the bench to give it another shot.

"MONSTER!" Arthur had already closed half the gap between him and FBP before Excalibur was unsheathed.

FBP shook his head sadly, but understood many of history's greatest scientists were persecuted for playing in what those of lesser intellect thought to be the world of the gods. Like Ben Franklin inventing lightning or the guy that turned Doritos into taco shells, he had just flown too close to the sun.

"I'll see myself out," FBP seethed, disgusted by the injustice, and threw himself into the portal.

FORMER BASEBALL PLAYER SUCKS AT CROWDFUNDING

Chapter Three

By Max Scoville (@MaxScoville)

The Year 1990

    Former Baseball Player hurdled through time and space, tachyons whizzing past him as he fell through the wormhole. Though moving at incomprehensible speeds, weaving a hectic path through across the fourth dimension, Former Baseball Player barely sensed he was moving; around him, entire lifetimes flitted before his eyes in a heartbeat, and civilizations rose and fell in a matter of seconds. Then, suddenly, with a flash, the blurred maelstrom was replaced with a cold, grey winter morning -- and Former Baseball Player found himself falling through midair!
    Trees, houses, cars, and the streets below came flying toward him. Former Baseball Player howled and flailed wildly, like a cat thrown in the bath. There was no way out of this one, and death seemed imminent. The retired athlete steeled himself and closed his eyes. If these were his last moments, he'd spend them right: dwelling on all the people who'd ever wronged him in the slightest, and hating them as much as possible. "Fuck all these assholes," he thought, as the face of just about everyone he'd ever met flashed before his eyes. "I hope they fall out of the sky, too, right into their own asses." Then, Former Baseball Player felt a strong jerk,

his head spun, and he heard a loud ripping sound. He kept his eyes closed. "So this is death," he thought. "It's a cold day in hell indeed."

"HEY MISTER, I CAN SEE YOUR WIENER!" a shrill voice cried. Former Baseball Player snapped his eyes open to see a small boy. Former Baseball Player realized he was in someone's front yard, in what appeared to be an upper middle-class suburban neighborhood. A thick layer of snow covered everything, and there were Christmas lights on the trees, plastic snowmen and Santa Clauses in front of neighboring houses. The young boy was standing on the sidewalk wearing a winter coat and a knitted hat with a pom-pom on top. He had mittens pinned to his sleeves. He must've been about eight years old.

Former Baseball Player looked up to see what had saved him. By some stroke of luck, his pants had snagged and had ripped completely off, breaking Former Baseball Player's fall. Unfortunately, this also left his wiener hanging out for any passers-by to see. Had Former Baseball Player been graced with a normal-sized penis, this wouldn't have fazed him, but his was so small that exposing it to cold temperatures risked it shriveling up completely, sucking itself into his body cavity like a salted snail, where it would atrophy and become even more useless than it already was. As it was exceptionally cold out, Former Baseball Player's penis was exceptionally tiny. Like, really, really tiny. In fact,

FORMER BASEBALL PLAYER SUCKS AT CROWDFUNDING

it was amazing that this young boy could even see it from a distance.

That was the other thing about Former Baseball Player's penis: he hated when anyone looked at it. He hated when his teammates looked at it, in the Former Baseball Sports Locker Room, and he especially hated when women looked at it. In fact, the one time he'd tricked a woman into forgetting how revolting she found him, he'd made her wear a complex blindfold apparatus during sex, made from welding goggles with the lenses painted over, followed by a heavy wool scarf wrapped around her entire head, and then a hatbox over that. Now, here was this child, staring unabashedly at Former Baseball Player's biggest (or smallest) shame.

"DON'T YOU LOOK AT MY DICK, YOU SHITTY LITTLE FUCK, HOW DARE YOU!" Former Baseball Player howled at the youth, awkwardly shifting around in an attempt to cover himself, but only causing the tree branch to bob up and down, shaking snow onto his tiny penis.

"WHY DON'T YOU COME DOWN HERE AND MAKE ME, YOU COOZE!" the boy replied.

Former Baseball Player hated children. He hated them more than anything, since, after all, they were technically a cross between his two most hated things: women, and men with functional genitalia.

Former Baseball Player couldn't handle it any more, and flew into a blind rage, spinning his arms around like windmills, humping the air wildly. His pants started to rip again. The boy noticed, and started walking away, carrying his two plastic bags of groceries.

"I'm gonna come find you, you little shit!" Former Baseball Player growled. "...And when I do, I'm gonna make you EAT MY ASS!"

"Gross!" said the boy. Then his grocery bags broke, spilling his food all over the sidewalk. At the same time, Former Baseball Player's pants ripped clean off, dropping him like a ton of bricks onto a snow-covered doghouse below. The doghouse shattered, and Former Baseball Player howled in agony. The young boy abandoned his groceries and took off running.

Former Baseball Player picked himself up and ran to the boy's abandoned groceries. He began hurling boxes of macaroni and cans of soup after him.

"I HOPE YOU STARVE TO DEATH, YOU DICK-LOOKING BRAT! I'M GONNA FUCK UP ALL YOUR SHITTY FOOD NOW!" he screamed, stomping the package of pudding into the ground. But the boy was out of sight. Just then, Former Baseball Player heard an engine approaching from the opposite direction. In the interest of modesty, he tore open a cereal box, emptied out an egg carton, and using these and the ripped plastic bags, he fashioned a crude but effective diaper; like fashionable European-style briefs, but made out of garbage.

A van turned a corner and Former Baseball Player tried to look casual, standing on

FORMER BASEBALL PLAYER SUCKS AT CROWDFUNDING

the street, surrounded by foodstuffs in his homemade underwear. The van rolled to a stop and the passenger-side window rolled down. A small, chubby man in a knit cap leaned out. Behind the wheel, a gangly, bearded man was looking at him, wide-eyed.

"Ah...Happy Holidays!" Former Baseball Player called out, rubbing his hands together in the cold. "How about this snow?" The chubby man grinned at him, and a gold tooth twinkled. "Say, you gentlemen wouldn't happen to know what year it is, would you?" The chubby man looked at his partner, and back at Former Baseball Player.

"What YEAR? You don't know what YEAR it is?" he asked, incredulously

"Yeah, I'm uh. I'm REAL DRUNK," replied Former Baseball Player, mentally congratulating himself for such quick thinking.

"It's 1990. Christmas Eve." The skinny guy in the driver's seat leaned over and muttered something to him. "...Herb, shut the fuck up, you don't give orders," the chubby man snapped at him. He turned back to Former Baseball Player. "You didn't happen to see a little kid around here, did you? Maybe about eight years old, carrying some groceries?"

Former Baseball Player flew into a rage again.

"You better believe I did, and I'm gonna kill him, too. I'm gonna kill that kid, for looking at my dick. I'm gonna burn that kid's goddamn house down."

The two men in the van looked at each other hesitantly. The chubby one looked around cautiously.

"Well, I'm Barry, and this is Herb," the chubby guy began, before Herb interjected.

"We're the Soggy Outlaws. We rob people, and then we clog the sinks and flood the..." Herb's sentence was cut short by Barry punching him hard in the arm.

"What my esteemed colleague means to say is that we've taken a, shall we say... particular interest in that boy, as we believe that he's been left unsupervised for the holidays," Barry grinned. "So, we've taken it upon ourselves to relieve him of some of his valuables, tomorrow night. Would you care you accompany us?"

"I would be delighted," Former Baseball Player said happily, "as long as we can burn his house down afterwards. For looking at my dick."

Barry and Herb laughed heartily.

"Hop in. The more the merrier," Barry said.

"Well, it looks like it'll be a Merry Christmas after all."

Every part of the robbery went according to plan. Everything, at least, up until the part where Barry, Herb, and Former Baseball Player broke into the boy's house to steal his family's things. That's when everything went sideways. The three would-be robbers sat huddled in a corner of the basement. During the course of the break-in, the boy had shot Herb in the eye with

FORMER BASEBALL PLAYER SUCKS AT CROWDFUNDING

an air rifle, and it seemed pretty likely he wouldn't see out of that eye again. He'd lost his shoes after stepping on roofing tar, and after attempting to proceed stocking-footed, he'd impaled one foot on a nail, getting shards of broken glass Christmas ornaments lodged in his hands and feet. Following that, he'd gone into shock.

Barry and Former Baseball Player tried another route into the house, but didn't have much success either after the boy hurled full paint cans down the stairs at them. Former Baseball Player had only been grazed by a gallon of Benjamin Moore "Polar Lights" beige, but Barry had sustained a visibly broken nose after making direct contact with a full can of "Autumn Bronze" tan, followed closely by one of "Candle White," which left him dazed and incoherent.

Former Baseball Player helped Barry down the stairs, carefully avoiding the upturned nail, the roofing tar, and Herb's shoes.

"Uhnghum neener honsapul," mumbled Barry, as they reached the bottom step. Blood gushing out of his nose, Former Baseball Player helped him down alongside Herb.

"Yeah, you're GODDAMN RIGHT we're gonna kill that little fuckin' kid. First he stares at my cock, and then he hurts my..." he was cut short by Barry vomiting into his lap.

"Ahgh need HOBSITAL" gagged Barry. Former Baseball Player noticed that Barry's gold tooth had been knocked out.

Former Baseball Player hated hospitals, and doctors too, for that matter; they always tried to look at his dick. Medical professionals were all a bunch of dirty dick-lookers. He glanced down to make sure his homemade underwear was still covering him, and it was. Michael Jordan grinned up him from his Wheaties-box codpiece. Barry and Herb had offered him some pants, but he didn't want them to see his tiny penis while he was changing, so he politely said no thank you.

From upstairs, the boy's voice rang out.

"I'm up here, you horse's ass! Come and get me!" and then after a brief pause, Bobby Helms' *Jingle Bell Rock* started playing on a stereo, somewhere on the other side of the house.

"I'll jingle your bells, you little buttfucker, I'll jingle your bells when I burn your fucking house down," growled Former Baseball Player. He looked around the basement. Barry and Herb weren't in very good shape. Herb had stopped breathing, and Barry had pissed himself. Former Baseball Player shook his head. What a waste of perfectly good violent criminals.

In one corner of the basement were a washer and dryer. Former Baseball Player walked over to them. Sure enough, behind the dryer was a hose leading to a gas line. He grabbed it firmly and tugged as hard as his could. Immediately there was a soft hiss and the smell of gas. He hurried over Barry and Herb, and crouched in front of them.

FORMER BASEBALL PLAYER SUCKS AT CROWDFUNDING

"Don't worry, boys, Former Baseball Player will save you!" he said as he positioned himself between the robbers, prepared to drag them out to the street. Then, one of the plastic bags holding his homemade underpants together tore, and the whole thing fell to the ground. There was Former Baseball Player, crouched, naked from the waist down.

Herb, who was apparently not actually dead, stirred. His one functional eye opened and he looked at Former Baseball Player. Then his gaze lowered.

"Oh my god..." he said in a hoarse whisper, "that's the smallest penis I've ever seen. BARRY, LOOK AT THIS GUY'S HILARIOUS BABYDICK!" He nudged Barry, who opened his eyes half way. Then, all the way. Then, he sat up a little bit, completely forgetting his concussion and broken nose.

"Former Baseball Player, what the hell is that?" wheezed Barry. "You call that a dick? That's not a dick, I don't even know what you'd call that!" Barry and Herb were in tears, laughing hysterically at Former Baseball Player's Greek tragedy of a schlong. It was the saddest penis they'd ever seen, and they couldn't contain themselves. Former Baseball Player was frozen, mortified, like a deer in headlights.

"FFF... FUCK YOU, FUCK B-BOTH OF YOU! JUST A COUPLE OF... DUMB, uh, TITS... IS WHAT YOU ARE," sputtered Former Baseball Player, who really had fallen quite a long way from his previous days as a professional athlete.

"Fuck us?" cackled Herb. "I don't know how you would, given your particular, uh, circumstances!" He and Barry wheezed with laughter as Former Baseball Player backed slowly to the door. "You have a very small penis, Former Baseball Player!" coughed Herb. Blood drizzled from Barry's broken nose. Former Baseball Player had enough. He shouldn't have to put up with this, he should be the kind of guy who dates sexy ladies, like Hooters waitresses, not the kind of guy whose genitals get made fun of by felons!

By the basement door, Former Baseball Player found a can of kerosene. He splashed it all over the basement as the two crooks continued to call him names like "teeny weenie," "baby dick," and "squirrel penis," but Former Baseball Player didn't care. He was in a blind rage. Maybe it was the time travel, maybe it was the long history of steroid use, but he was a whirlwind of hate. A whirlwind of hate that would never properly please a woman, on account of the small penis.

Former Baseball Player walked backwards up the steps leading outside, leaving a trail of kerosene behind him. From inside the house, he heard "Jingle Bell Rock" stop and then start again for what seemed like the fifth time. In the window, he could see the silhouette of the awful young boy, dancing with what appeared to be a cardboard cutout of Michael Jordan. "Fuck this house," he thought. "Fuck this whole house full of dick-looking shitheads. The kid, Barry,

FORMER BASEBALL PLAYER SUCKS AT CROWDFUNDING

Herb...Cardboard Michael Jordan... Fuck all of you."

Then, he lit a match and tossed it toward the basement steps.

Under normal circumstances, the blast from an exploding suburban basement full of pressurized gas and kerosene vapors from the distance of a few meters would kill a man, even a man with a background in professional sports. But at that exact moment, the time-vortex opened again, and Former Baseball Player was instantaneously pulled away as the entire house erupted into flame.

DAN RYCKERT AND FRIENDS

FORMER BASEBALL PLAYER SUCKS AT CROWDFUNDING

Chapter Four

By Mitch Dyer (@MitchyD)

The Year 33

The ferocious heat of a new world attacked Former Baseball Player's body as he burst through another tear in time.

As he tumbled down onto the coarse, sandy surface of this unknown place, he had but one desire. The icon felt, with a desperation he'd never known, the urge to strike back against the oppressive warmth and blinding brightness of this new world. If it stopped cowering in the depths of space, the sun wouldn't stand a chance in a one-on-one fight against the black-belt martial arts expert.

As his aging eyes adjusted to the light and he began pulling himself off the ground, FBP realized his clothes didn't make the jump through time. Crouching on the ground, completely nude in the smoky haze where the collapsing portal once was, his mind leapt to *Terminator 2*. "I look just like Arnold Schwarzenegger did," he thought, "Only more muscular and successful." He indulged the fantasy for a long while, imagining cameras surrounding him as he often thought they should, bringing himself to a world in utter disbelief of his 250 pounds of pure muscle.

A voice shattered Former Baseball Player's mental recreation of *Terminator 2*.

"Please," said a soft-spoken man, "Let me help you, friend."

FBP stood, his 6'4" frame dwarfing the filthy, bearded man in front of him.

"Don't be stupid," the giant said. "I'm Former Baseball Player, a former baseball player, and I don't need help from a homeless idiot like you. Get out of my face and go eat some trash."

Before the former athlete could turn away, the small, sweaty man was already disrobing, doing his best to shield his naked body from the eyes of a growing, whispering crowd. "Please," the man said again, "Take this, I'd like you to have it."

The dirt-speckled robe was the opposite of comfortable, and didn't fit Former Baseball Player whatsoever. Although he would never admit it to this stranger, FBP felt grateful. After years of internalizing the shame, exposing his humiliating penis to his fellow baseball players or the public was his deepest fear. FBP took a moment to process the generosity of a man who now stood naked before the crowd. As his hairy new friend guided him away from the chattering mass and into what must have been his home, Former Baseball Player had three simultaneous epiphanies.

First, he realized he had arrived in Jerusalem.

Secondly, the kind-spirited but disgusting man who swept him off the street had a penis

FORMER BASEBALL PLAYER SUCKS AT CROWDFUNDING

that Former Baseball Player could only describe as tremendous, easily five, perhaps even six times the size of his stubby stump.

Third, as he sat at a table of 12, and Mark, Luke, and a bunch of other guys whose names he instantly forgot introduced themselves, FBP realized that this hippie hobo burnout could only be Jesus Christ.

"Listen, little buddy," FBP said as Jesus refilled his wine chalice, "I'm glad you gave me a shirt, but I have to go. When I jumped off that bridge, I thought I had nothing to live for, but that's because I totally forgot about the home run competition on Tuesday, and I have world records to shatter. Did I tell you I can smash a ball 500 feet into the bleachers?"

Judas, exhausted by this guest's rambling, stood and abruptly left the room, mumbling something to himself.

"Don't mind Judas," said Jesus. "He means well, and in his soul, he is a good man." The remaining 11 men nodded in approval.

Former Baseball Player snorted. "As an atheist-Scientologist, I've done my research on all of these dumb religious cults, Jesus. I can tell you right now, that dude is a douche. Anyone with common sense knows he's going to sell you out to that Greek guy from Monty Python."

"I do not know a Monty Python," said Mark, "does he work with Pontius Pilate?"

"Who the hell is Pontius Pilate?" Former Baseball Player asked through a mouthful of stale bread.

Jesus smiled, finished his drink, and rose from his seat. He wished everyone well, thanked them for their company at dinner, and asked FBP to join him outside. Hoping that perhaps he'd find a portal home hidden in the garden, he followed Jesus out the dilapidated door.

"You are a strange man, Former Baseball Player," said Jesus, "but that is what defines you. We have not known each other long, but I can tell that, wherever you're from, people want to know what you have to say. I admire this, and hope that anything I teach has the influence of your voice."

"Yeah, I have a ton of Twitter followers and I'm probably going to be the Mayor of Quebec in like a year."

"You're a leader? That's inspirational. I wish we could have known each other sooner. You would have been able to help Paul greatly. We could have spoken about the greatness inside everyone. We could have reached more people sooner, spread our message together."

"Yeah, whatever. Was your mom really a virgin, buddy? That shit is driving me crazy."

The perplexed look on Jesus' face vanished as Judas emerged at the edge of the garden.

"Ah, there you are, Judas," said Jesus, who strode toward his friend. Former Baseball Player watched the two discuss something, but

FORMER BASEBALL PLAYER SUCKS AT CROWDFUNDING

didn't particularly care what either of them had to say. The two men drew closer, and the conversation carried the same sort of intensity Former Baseball Player brought when he wanted to bust out some of his sick black belt skills on someone.

Judas leaned into Jesus' ear, whispered something, and kissed his face. Former Baseball Player, confused, remembered learning that Jesus didn't have a romantic life, not even with Mary Magdalene. "Now I know more about Jesus than anyone," he thought.

As Judas turned his back, a small squadron of soldiers strode into the garden. They announced that they'd be arresting Jesus, and stopped speaking when they saw an unfamiliar and disheveled man towering above them. The man obviously in command of the group consulted Judas. "Arrest him, too. He's been conspiring with this one the entire time. He's equally responsible, in fact."

Former Baseball Player, still wondering if Jesus and Judas were dating, or something, didn't hear the comment, nor Jesus' rebuttal to protect him. The commander approached FBP and drew his sword while his men dragged Jesus away.

When Former Baseball Player realized what was happening, he rolled up his sleeves.

"I know a bunch of martial arts, I'm an expert and I have black belts," Former Baseball Player said. "I know stuff that doesn't exist yet. I fight in MMA and will crush you with my biceps.

I'll hit your head 500 feet away like you're a baseball. Everyone thinks I should have been in *Terminator 2*. I guarantee that you'll regret messing with me."

The intimidating behemoth took a step forward. The soldier took a step back.

"I'm Former Baseball Player. I dare you to fight me, bud."

When he woke up, FBP could barely see Jesus through the blood in his eyes. He tried to get up, but discovered his hands were tied to a board laid across his back. He stood up and spun around, trying to gain his bearings, but the heavy wooden cross made it difficult to see.

Jesus stood, too, clearly struggling to keep his balance, his slender body barely supporting the monstrous weight of the wooden cross. FBP noticed a large crowd, and heard a thunderous snap drown out their cheering, chanting, and shouting.

Jesus dropped to the ground, the whiplash leaving a vicious mark across his back. Jesus stood again, walked just two steps, and collapsed as another blow struck him.

Again, he rose.

FBP decided to prove a point to their captors and the world around them. He'd dealt with worse in the ring, he thought, and as the single toughest man he could think of, Former Baseball Player decided he'd carry the cross and endure the attacks. He'd do it better than Jesus, and he'd make it to the end of the path first,

FORMER BASEBALL PLAYER SUCKS AT CROWDFUNDING

showing his true strength. As he took his first step, FBP dropped to one knee, his feeble steroid-pumped body completely incapable of carrying the wood. When he tried to rise up, his legs gave out and his face smashed into the ground. Many mocked his weakness. Jesus continued to walk. FBP struggled to get up off the ground without the use of his arms, and before long, some sympathetic folks dragged him to the end of the path to catch up with Jesus. The two found themselves side by side as their crucifixes were lifted, planted into the ground, and displayed for a contentious crowd.

"Forgive them, father," Jesus said to the sky. "You too, Former Baseball Player. They know not what they do. Do not forsake your fellow man because he was raised without the knowledge of God's grace."

FBP passed out before he could tell Jesus to stop being a pussy.

He had hoped to awaken in a new time period, something better than this dirty, smelly place without bathrooms, showers, toothbrushes, or body-enhancing narcotics. He couldn't see a thing in the dark, and thought he'd gone blind when Jesus explained they'd been locked in a cave for a few days. Both men lost consciousness on their crosses, Jesus explained, but they'd survived.

"The power of the Lord, our God, gave us the strength to persevere, my friend" said Jesus. "And soon He will liberate us and bring us to His kingdom. You did a powerful, wonderful thing for the world on that cross, Former Baseball Player."

"I did?"

"Yes. The world will remember our sacrifice and what we endured for them for the rest of time. It will make this world a better place."

"This place sucks."

Suddenly, a piercing white light assaulted their eyes. "The portal! Finally, I can get out of this trash dump," FBP said.

His heart sank when the apostles emerged from the light. They helped FBP and Jesus to their feet and carried them beyond the walls of their mountainside tomb before putting the boulder back in its place. FBP was exhausted, smelled like his own piss, and felt weary from having his ass repeatedly kicked by the Biblical era.

"You are both blessed!" Luke said. "Praise God for this resurrection."

"God doesn't give you erections," FBP said. He began wondering where boners came from, and stopped paying attention to everything. He became lost in thought for some time, wondering if his penis was, in fact, capable of defying gravity, or if it was actually capable of flight.

Former Baseball Player became aware of the world again when two golden beams of light shot down from the sky and ensconced he and Jesus. It felt warm, made his entire body tingle, which didn't help him hide the stiffy he'd been trying to keep secret while he thought about

FORMER BASEBALL PLAYER SUCKS AT CROWDFUNDING

boner science. FBP felt weightless as his body glided off the ground, and he realized that God was pulling him, alongside Jesus, into Heaven. The two floated upward, silently staring at each other.

"Heaven is a wonderful place. You've earned your place in the kingdom of virgins, fine wines, perfect people, and infinite pleasure," the Son of God said.

For the first time, Former Baseball Player shed his existing beliefs, and was in awe of the power of Christ. The man had a convincing, strong voice to help sell the ideals of the religion he'd spawn. Even though Former Baseball Player loathed the idea of religion, especially those he wasn't part of, he was pretty pumped about heaven. If he'd never make it back to his time, if he'd never make the home run competition, if he'd never be able to beat up his nemesis Dan Ryckert, Former Baseball Player could accept the loss if the gain was happiness in the Heavenly Kingdom of God.

"Thank you, Jesus," he said.

They rose above the clouds, shooting faster and farther into the sky.

"Thank you, Former Baseball Player, for accepting me into your heart."

FBP looked up, and through the hole in the night, he could see the magnificent daytime blue of Heaven's sky piercing through the world. He felt whole for the first time in his life. He closed his eyes.

DAN RYCKERT AND FRIENDS

Former Baseball Player was about to go where he always knew he belonged.

FORMER BASEBALL PLAYER SUCKS AT CROWDFUNDING

Chapter Five

By Mikey Neumann (@mikeyface)

The Year 1888

What follows is an eyewitness account of a strange occurrence in the civil parish of Whitechapel in London's East End. The journal of Mason Fairfellatio was not discovered until 1954. It is believed to be one of the most accurate accounts of Jack the Ripper in the public record, but was discounted due to the peculiar way in which the Ripper talked and by a mysterious stranger that shows up in the following excerpted passage. It is shown here, in full, to let a discerning public decide the veracity of Mason's claims for themselves.

The East End is quiet this time of night. Families say rehearsed prayers and tuck away in their beds as the candles flicker out by the bedside. Once the working class are asleep, coping with the frigid October London air, the ladies of Whitechapel go to work. Nearly 1,200 women, cooped up in 62 brothels, take to the streets to earn a living in the oldest profession in the world. They have sex for money.

I've been following the Ripper for weeks now, I do not believe he has been alerted to my presence. I know he will strike tonight. The air is right; there's an odor of horse droppings and drunkards' post-coital fluids that I believe the Ripper finds captivating. He partook in a couple rounds of Rosemary Port in a local tavern called The Crumbling Giraffe, where I stepped in, unbeknownst to him, and saved him quite the beating at the hands of street thugs. You see, Rosemary Port is known as quite the "poofter drink" around here and its most common use is for inebriating crying infants. When the Ripper was questioned about his drink, he yelled "Get crunk, balls out; it's Miller time!" and hit his head rather deftly upon the countertop. He then added, "Ain't nobody in here wanna step to this!"

    He speaks in the most curious idiosyncrasies.

    I've been following him, careful to disappear into shadow when he takes a moment to gander at his surroundings, for hours now. The selection was made, a dirty-blonde from "The Horse-Drawn Congress Carriage," or as it's known around this parish, "The Bang Wagon." She is fair-skinned, probably twenty-two years of age but looks at least forty—probably due to the opiate-fueled potassium deficiencies emblematic of Whitechapel. It is colloquial knowledge that one should not eat the bananas sold in the markets here. I would elaborate further, but suffice to say, any market that will put produce out "on loan" only to be returned at sunrise and sold forthwith, are a danger to one's venereal health.

    The Ripper moves in for conversation, caressing her crimson cheek. It's clear this

FORMER BASEBALL PLAYER SUCKS AT CROWDFUNDING

woman has been hard at work for hours now, fading in and out of consciousness as he effuses quandary-upon-quandary about the finer usages of medical equipment in a gentleman's bedroom. She appears unimpressed, pulling the conversation back to the financial transaction at hand, listing a rehearsed menu of slang expressions for varied sexual acts.

I pause behind a bin of rubbish, pontificating on what a "reverse-reverse-reverse-slug-jagger with a chowder finish" could possibly mean to describe. After a moment, I lean out, just a bit, to gaze upon the current calamity.

One of his many scalpels enters her neck. She falls like a bag of millweed onto the street as her eyes glaze into oblivion. At first I'm not certain, but I hypothesize that she sees me, peering from the refuse like an inquiring rodent as her blood poured forth from her artery. The dying woman struggles to communicate as the Ripper begins his ghastly work on her abdominal region. I am nauseated. She gasps in my direction; I know in the definitive that she sees me now. Her eyes are accusatory and forlorn; that in her final moments a man with a hastily scribbled notebook chose to chronicle the final moments of her existence in lieu of running to her aid. My dear madam, there are no words to effectively parlay the appropriate regret for my steadfast lack of action. But I digress all too comfortably, albeit unfortunately, that there is nary a proper reason for both of us to perish under this desolate midnight. The Ripper would make short work of my rickets-ravaged bones. Be merry, my dear lady, that I will catch this sordid murderer and your sacrifice will be celebrated when he is run through the streets, adorned with the infuriated tomatoes and lettuce hurtled from the balconies of retribution.

"Girl," he speaks aloud as she fades at last into the great unknown; her eyes come to a close. "Girrrrrrl," he repeats, elongating the "ur" sound like he is suffering a maniacal spell as my Uncle Chesterbane did when a blood clot took to his brain. "You fiiiine," he elongates again. His speech patterns remain a fertile mystery to me. "Get money! Get money! Get money!" he repeats over-and-over as he tosses entrails into the frigid air, as if an enraged marsupial raging against his captivity.

All at once, I am terrified.

I fall against the wall and tremble as the shame of her death weighs deeply upon me.

Thunder strikes overhead yet I see no lightning. It baffles Ripper much the same. He pauses, taking a seat on the worn cobblestones in the alleyway, looking up to the stars he believes to be the only witness to his brazen insanity.

The thunder blares angrily once more, echoing through our narrow causeway. As before, there is no lightning. What witchcraft is afoot on this innocuous night? Perhaps our Lord has intervened, finally putting an end to the archaic blasphemy carved into the street urchins of our once great city. I say a prayer, asking

FORMER BASEBALL PLAYER SUCKS AT CROWDFUNDING

forgiveness for my own paltry inaction in the face of such evil. The Ripper takes to his feet—

[*There are three lines of text that could not be properly transcribed here. Mason scribbled a series of lines and exclamation points that do not appear to be any written language known to us. In all likeliness, he was so taken by the events that followed, he moved his pen around in terror. He then added exclamation points to it, posthumously.*]

    This light—
    It is blinding—
    Take me, oh, Lord. Take me into thine arms and I will accept the punishment that awaits my fragile cowardice. I am ready and willing to—
    Wait. Hold that thought, oh, Lord.
    A man fell from the light. He looks to have danced with the demons of alcoholism on this night—he is utterly, unapologetically drunk. This is not my Lord, not by any amalgamation of scripture known to me.
    This man is dressed in tattered gypsy clothing that I've never before laid my eyes upon. He is a witch, of this much, I am certain. He discharges a heinous belch and flatulates, brushing away hurriedly at the encrusted vomit running down his gypsy-blouse. He speaks. "Oh, dammit. Where am I now?"
    The light collapses unto itself, like a wave receding from the beachhead.

Ripper takes a step away from the man that fell from the light, covering his nose for a moment as the stench wanes into the atmosphere—the air is palatable again. I know of nothing I have in common with the Ripper, but I know the both of us wish beyond reason that the gypsy does not blow this gaseous horror from any orifice a second time. Did he, at the behest of his witch-at-arms, ingest the indignity better left to rest in a watercloset? Even at twenty-five paces, his breath is merciless.

The gypsy attempts to steady himself against the bricks of a row house, but trips on the eviscerated remains of the night madam. His eyes grow effulgent as he takes in the scandal beneath him. "Whoa. Gross. Is this Detroit—are we in Detroit?"

The Ripper cups a blade in his palm, concealing a righteous implement to strike the Gypsy down, should his hand be forced in this tense altercation. "Yo, what's your name, playa?" Ripper says.

"Uh," the Gypsy looks again to the deceased matron of sexual perversion. "I am a player, yes. I played baseball." He struggles with uncertain vomit as it cackles from his sternum to his mouth; he swallows it. "Are you Barry Sanders?"

"Hell naw," Ripper replies. "Ain't nobody holler at me by that name, dude. Are you drunk, homie?"

"Yes. Yes. Yup," the Gypsy says in rejoinder.

FORMER BASEBALL PLAYER SUCKS AT CROWDFUNDING

Ripper steps into the moonlight, giving the mysterious and inebriated Gypsy a clearer view of his face. "I am known as Jake. Jake the Ripper."

I wonder, still concealed like a refugee in the garbage, if he introduced himself incorrectly on purpose or if he truly does not know that the papers have labeled him "Jack the Ripper." At this moment, it occurs to me that his name might actually be "Jake."

The Gypsy exhales with closed eyes, held sturdy against the bricks. "Most people just call me Former Baseball Player. I'm famous—I'm super famous. I have a Twitter account with more followers than Lance Bass, bro."

Perhaps this "Twitter" is a Newspaper in Detroit. I will research this further at my earliest convenience. It would give me piece-of-mind to know what this strange man, now known to me as "Former Baseball Player", is talking about.

"Aight, I feel ya—I feel ya. Sucks that I probably gotta kill ya, former playa. Just how it is, naw-mean?" Ripper says.

Mr. Player seems unfazed by the suggested attack. "I just wanna know how to get out of here—where is here, by the way?"

"You in London, homie. That light thing you did was tight as hell. You were all like BAH-BLOAW SUCKA and landed right where I was doing my thaaaaang," Ripper was once again elongating his phrases. Perhaps he did it to defuse any would be attackers into thinking he was mentally unstable?

"What year?"

Ripper cocked his head in confusion. "What you mean, what year? It's 1888, playa. Holler atcha boy."

"Crap," Mr. Player said.

"Crap is right. It's about to get weiiiiiiiird up in here," Ripper said.

The Former Baseball Gypsy stood up against the wall, it appeared he had just come to a realization of some kind. "You're that dude that, like, killed all those hooker-broads aren't you?"

Ripper raised an eyebrow. "Oh, I'm all about that 'hooker' thing. Shit sounds cool as shit! I'ma steal that. Errbody gonna call me 'Jake the Hooker' from now. That's hot, man." He finished by making a series of deep spitting noises into his fist; it seemed to create a rhythm of some kind until he yelled "Drop!" rather loudly and proceeded to make a series of "Bwomp" noises.

"You just murdered this chick, didn't you?" The Gypsy asked, referencing the deceased madam at his feet.

"Hells to the yeah! She was eyeballin' me, like, wassup, you can come get it, playa. And I was all, I'ma cut this lady up because that's how I get mah rocks off, naw-mean?" Ripper said. I'm afraid I might have written it down wrong, but that's what it appeared to me was said. None of those words appear to fit together into a coherent thought. I'll examine further later.

FORMER BASEBALL PLAYER SUCKS AT CROWDFUNDING

"Do you really talk like that?" The Gypsy asked, echoing my own thoughts on the matter.

"Yup."

The Former Baseball Gypsy looked up and down the alleyway, probably in an effort to alert a law enforcement officer. "I'm gonna go, okay?"

Ripper brandished the blade in his palm in a threatening manner. "Naw, man. Can't letcha do that, homie."

This upset the Gypsy; he was visibly unnerved with his life being threatened.

"Dude, I will knock you the hell out."

"Raise up, playboy-ee," Ripper replied. He tossed the scalpel to the ground and brought his arms up to engage in a bout of fisticuffs with the Gypsy.

The Gypsy threw a strong right cross, which Ripper easily dodged to the side, leaving Mr. Player off-balance. Ripper gave a swift boot to the posterior, sending his attacker tumbling to the street. The inebriated Gypsy rose once more to his cleated boot, cracking his neck in a show of physical prowess.

"Lucky shot," Mr. Player said.

Ripper scoffed.

"I have more Twitter followers than Lance Bass, dude." He repeated.

"Yeah, dog, you already said that," Ripper laughed.

The Gypsy moved in slower this time, his arms up in the defensive fighting posture. He tried a few quick jabs, which Ripper continued to dodge with what appeared to be little effort.

Perhaps this "Lance Bass" is a fisherman of some acclaim that people trade tales of across the ocean in the United States?

They continued in their balletic trades of pugilistic wherewithal. The Gypsy seemed unable to land even a single blow to the sadistic murderer prancing around him in circles. "Whatchu got, homeboy? Come at me! Come at me, son!" Ripper shouted as the Former Baseball Gypsy grew more and more tired.

The Gypsy threw a monstrous right cross, missing by an unspeakable distance. Ripper dropped down and came back up with a vicious haymaker, planting it right under the Gypsy's chin. The sound was a ghastly, echoing crack, like a petard went off in the alleyway. It sent Mr. Player into the wall and plummeting to his trousers. It was the decisive blow.

"Game recognize game, son!" Ripper shouted repeatedly at his fallen attacker, like boisterous poetry relayed in unfamiliar quatrain. The game *indeed*, did recognize game.

The Gypsy moaned and took again to his feet, his hands up in defeat, bargaining with mumbled epithets to the murderer that bested him to cease their engagement. Many of the swears that spilled from his lips were phrases that I have never heard before. Surprisingly, the Ripper helps Former Baseball Gypsy to his feet, even dusting him off in the most gentlemanly of manners. For a moment, there is ease between them.

FORMER BASEBALL PLAYER SUCKS AT CROWDFUNDING

"Alright, pop 'em off. Lemme check out your gear." Ripper says, picking up his scalpel from the blood-soaked cobble of the alley.

"What?" The Gypsy says, rubbing the sides of his head.

"Get them trousers off, boy. Let's see what I got to work with here."

"What?" The Gypsy said again.

The Ripper sighed, quite audibly. "I wanna see the trouser meat. The bean spleen. The yogurt baby. The snakey-snake. The veined eruption. The gear. The package. The spurting jester. The boing-boing. The mango mustard. The cheeky purveyor of fine goods and services. The D. The P for the V. The P for the B. The P to the M to the V to the B and back to the V again." He said that all in one breath. "Dog, lemme see that Bavarian Knackwurst with a sauerkraut delivery system!"

"Dude, you want me to take my pants off?" The Gypsy was understandably filled with confusion. I do believe the Ripper was asking, albeit in a flurry of non-sequiter, to see Mr. Player's princess-pleaser, as we're known to say around these parts.

"Rip out the gear or I'll rip 'em out for ya, playa."

"Come on, dude. I've had a horrible day. I suck at everything. Seriously, pick anything and I suck at it." The Gypsy looked like he was about to collapse in a flurry of effeminate tears. "Leave me this one thing, man."

"No can do, shorty. Gots to get my mutilation on, nawm-sayin'? Whip the bits; roll-em' out!" Ripper pointed the scalpel at the Gypsy's throat.

"Son of a bitch," Mr. Player whispered to himself as he struggled with his remarkably small belt buckle. "Don't laugh, I was swimming, uh, and it was cold, where..." he was clearly making this up. "...where I was swimming. It was really cold and I was just swimming in the cold water. Where it was cold. In the water."
The Gypsy dropped his trousers and undergarments.

Laughter followed, both mercilessly from the Ripper and from my own person, covering my mouth to stifle the wandering gasps of guffawed racket.

"I don't even know what to do with that, son," Ripper said, drowning in his own laughter. "That shit looks like somebody stepped on a couple grapes and glued it back together. You ain't pleasin' no lady with that disaster, homie."

The Gypsy hurriedly pulled his trousers back to his waist. "Ha ha. Yeah, laugh it up. It's all very funny," he said with observable sarcasm.

Thunder again roared overhead.

"Oh, thank god," the Gypsy said to himself as Ripper readied his blade to strike.

"Just gonna put you outta your misery, playa." Ripper lunged forward with his scalpel toward the trachea of the Gypsy.

FORMER BASEBALL PLAYER SUCKS AT CROWDFUNDING

The bright light flashed again and the scalpel collided with the wall, bending it sideways and spiraling to the ground.

Ripper looked around in confusion. The Gypsy had dissipated into the musky twilight of London's East End.

Just as the mysterious Gypsy witch had appeared, he disappeared in exactly the same way.

I am still keenly concealed behind the rubbish cart, watching the Ripper abandon his nightly kill and pack up his tools of mutilation into a leather satchel. He walks away into the darkness covering the other end of the alleyway.

It is my belief, that in the future, this journal, my longest and most intriguing run-in with the Ripper yet, will be discounted on the grounds that none of this can be true to the reality of this world. Gypsy witches do not simply appear out of thin air and engage with the most infamous serial killer of my time. Alas, should it take me the rest of my days, I will uncover the identity of the traveling Gypsy and assuage myself of any charges that the masses will trump upon me for what they will believe to be a fiction.

I will stay hidden for another twenty minutes before I travel home, surely unable to sleep when I think back on the events of this midnight encounter with the Devil and a witch who called himself "Former Baseball Player."

I pray we meet again, Gypsy.

DAN RYCKERT AND FRIENDS

FORMER BASEBALL PLAYER SUCKS AT CROWDFUNDING

Chapter Six

By Tim Ryder (@timryder)

The Year 1933

The girl was beautiful. Hair, red like rubies. Skin as smooth and creamy as milk. And not that skim bullshit. The good kind – the kind that tasted great even as you knew it was bad for you. She was wearing a red dress, which you would think would be too much red with her hair and all, but it wasn't. Yeah, she was beautiful all right. The kind of beautiful that made you wish she wasn't dead. But she was. Dead, I mean. But also beautiful. Beautiful and dead.

She was also covered in blood. That <u>was</u> way too much red.

The early morning fog settled over the harbor like gravy on mashed potatoes. Mashed potatoes so smooth and delicious and yet deceptive, so when you take your first bite you're like, "Oh, these are garlic mashed potatoes HELL YES."

I began to think I was hungry.

I'd been called out to the docks by my old friend Detective Hawkins. He often called for my help when cases took a turn for the bizarre. He had his hands more than full chasing bootleggers and appreciated the extra pair of eyes. And since I was often drunk enough to be seeing double, my eyes were extra useful.

The girl was splayed out near the end of the dock, her eyes looking out to sea like she was just waiting for her ship to come in. I guess, in a way, it already had. It just wasn't the ship she was expecting. Instead of a beautiful pleasure cruise, it was a grisly murder ship. The kind of mix-up that'll make you find a new travel agent. Still, the way her green eyes were looking out at the horizon – it was almost peaceful, like in her last moment she had found some semblance of –

"Whoa this dead chick has a sweet rack...what a waste."

I was snapped out of my reverie as I often was, by the insensitive ramblings of Former Baseball Player, my new partner. Partner maybe isn't the right word – it implies a sort of intellectual parity that I can assure you was in no way present. He was a partner in the sense that a good dog is a partner, except a dog drooled less. He was a partner is the sense that a gun is a partner, except a gun was more reliable. He was a partner in the sense that...okay, he was a partner in exactly no sense at all.

But he was a huge brute of a man and made a decent bodyguard. He could snap a man's neck with his bare hands and would do so without a moment's thought. A thought, if that indeed was something he was interested in pursuing, would take a great deal longer than a moment.

I had met him a few weeks back at Charlie's, a local speakeasy that was one of my many watering holes. And when I say watering

FORMER BASEBALL PLAYER SUCKS AT CROWDFUNDING

hole, I'm using the term like an animal would. Sure, I drank there but I also occasionally slept on a small bed of leaves. I was just shaping a few leaves into the general shape of a pillow when I heard FBP boasting about his baseball career and how he was better than Babe Ruth. Through some smooth talking and a few purchased drinks, I was able to calm the place down before a riot broke out. We got to talking and he started telling this crazy story of how he fell through a portal and ended up here. A story like that would often be followed with tight jackets and pleasant orderlies wearing all white, but I don't judge. I was born in Shreveport and originally wanted to be a floral designer. We all have our stories.

It was around then that Charlie started yelling at me about how when you say "the next round's on me," you actually have to pay for that round of drinks with money or some other acceptable currency. Not wanting to argue semantics, I beat a hasty retreat. I had made it all the way back to my office before I noticed FBP had followed me the whole way home, like a little lost puppy. A little lost giant asshole puppy. He's been with me ever since, partly because he's useful, partly because I'm not entirely sure he can survive without adult supervision and partly because I've got a thing for lost causes.

"whoa all this blood is this chick on her period someone get the midol lol."

Goddammit. Some people have no respect for a decent reverie.

"Okay, FBP," I said calmly. "Let's just look for the facts here. Remember, the facts lead to the truth and the truth leads to -"

"hamburgers lol."

"Getting paid," I said, shaking my head. "But close." Which wasn't really true. It was close in the way that Moscow and Chicago were close. They were on the same planet, but no one short of an idiot would try to drive between them. But FBP needed encouragement. Like a gorilla learning sign language, occasionally you give him a treat even if he signs "butt."

"That's strange," I said. "No sign of a struggle. This came as a surprise." I delicately rolled her over, like I was trying to escape a one-night stand without waking her. I was good at that. "Yep. There it is. Someone stabbed this girl in the back. Puncture wound, right under the rib cage. But not with a knife – the shape's wrong. It was something long and thin, like a screwdriver or a -"

"or a icicle perfect murder weapon just melts away no fingerprints lol."

Jesus Christ. An icicle. The first go-to of any amateur private eye. It's never an icicle. Never. It's completely impractical – how do you transport it? How do you get a decent grip on it? It's ice, for god's sake. But it doesn't stop morons from guessing it.

"Sure, FBP," I said. "We'll keep icicle on the list." Give the gorilla a treat for not throwing <u>all</u> his feces.

FORMER BASEBALL PLAYER SUCKS AT CROWDFUNDING

Hawkins finished up with the medical examiner and walked over. "Whaddya think, Mac?," he asked. My name was Joe McKinney, so it was technically an abbreviation and not just cool police slang. Enough people called me Mac that I thought about legally changing my name but then I'd be Mac McKinney and there are only so many hard k sounds one name can bear. I'd also briefly flirted with the idea of changing my name to Dick so I could tell people I was Dick the private dick but that was asinine. Now I had a deal with myself where every time I thought about changing my name, I took a drink and that seemed to work well.

"This girl's dead, Hawkins," I said.

"Crackerjack investigating as always, Mac," said Hawkins, cracking a smile but just barely. It was an old joke between us, dating back to our days on the force together. Before our lives took different paths.

"What's more, I know who she is. Her name is Savannah," I said, realizing that it had been a little tacky to refer to her as "the girl" this whole time when I knew damn well what her name was. Oh well. She wouldn't be taking offense anytime soon. "She's a singer down at The Silver Spoon. Good one too."

"Maybe someone didn't think so," said Hawkins.

"Hell of a bad review," I replied.

"yeah hell of a bad review what the hell its like dont like my singing okay but dont stab me geez lol"

"Pipe down, FBP. The grown-ups are talking," I said. "Why don't you go move those shipping crates around for a while." He dutifully did as he was told.

"He's really something," said Hawkins as he watched the brute go about the menial task with enthusiasm.

"Yeah," I replied. "My own private battleship, walking and talking. Kind of."

"So what do you think," asked Hawkins, our attention turning back to the still very-dead Savannah. "Robbery gone wrong?"

"A robbery doesn't make her come out to the docks in the middle of the night. Besides, she's a fine singer but she doesn't make that much money. No, this was someone she knew. You don't turn your back to a dangerous stranger."

"Love affair gone wrong, maybe?"

"Maybe. She's a heartbreaker, that's for sure. I'll ask around at The Silver Spoon, see if she had a fella."

"Or a crazed fan."

A shipping crate fell to the ground and splintered into pieces.

"what the fuck I guess you loose at jenga dude lol."

"Be careful with that one," said Hawkins. "I don't know if I trust him."

"Oh, I definitely don't," I said. "But I don't think I have a choice."

The fog got foggier.

FORMER BASEBALL PLAYER SUCKS AT CROWDFUNDING

The people at The Silver Spoon took the news about Savannah hard. Like a trail of ants crossing the highway, they didn't know what hit them. Breaking bad news was my least favorite part of the job, aside from the pay, the hours, and the job in general, but sometimes it seemed like it was all I did. I just kept reminding myself that the news was already broken – I was just relaying the message that it couldn't be fixed. It was small comfort and didn't make much sense, but sometimes, like a barn full of midgets in a tornado, you cling to the little things to survive.

What's worse is that in between the sobs, no one was able to tell me much of anything. Savannah was a good girl – came in, sang her songs, kept her nose clean and stayed out of trouble. No rivals, no jealous boyfriend, no one who would want her dead at all. I walked out with less than I had coming in. Although to be fair, I had purchased a few drinks, so my lighter wallet was my fault.

I'd gone back to my office to think. Try to make sense of it all. The flask was helping. FBP wasn't. He'd taken his pants off, something he did a lot in private and also pretty frequently in public. He was currently attempting to climb my filing cabinets like a dumbass. The gorilla analogy was looking more and more accurate. I was worried about the stability of the cabinets – they were empty, so they didn't have much weighing them down. I wasn't much for keeping files.

"Get down from there, you idiot," I said.

"haha im donkey kong get ready to jump some barrels lol"

At this point, I feel I should clarify that he was literally saying "el-oh-el" at the end of his sentences. It was super annoying. I was about to tell him as much when I heard a knock at the door.

It was quickly followed by a few more knocks, which was comforting. Just one knock would have been strange.

"Get down from there. And put some pants on. No one wants to see your tiny penis."

"hey fuck you i dont have a -"

"Yes, you do. You really do. I was going to make my next case figuring out what the hell happened to it but then I remembered I don't care. Put some damn pants on."

The knocks continued. I could see the silhouette of a woman behind the door. I'd seen plenty of silhouettes through that door. This was in the top 5. Maybe top 3. I decided to make opening the door a priority. After a couple attempts at the handle, I finally found purchase and swung the door open. Savannah briskly walked through.

This was surprising for several reasons.

"what the fuck how the hell did the dead chick just walk in zombie attack i guess lol."

The fact that FBP and I were on the same mental page chilled me to the bone.

"I imagine you have several questions, Mr. McKinney," said the somehow-walking around Savannah.

FORMER BASEBALL PLAYER SUCKS AT CROWDFUNDING

"Please, call me Mac. Most people do," I said, mostly on instinct.

"Well, Mac, before we get to those questions, I feel I must inform you that you have a large man with a tiny penis on top of your filing cabinets."

"hey fuck you zombie lady its not -"

"Unprompted, FBP!" I yelled, still baffled but glad to at least have an easy target for my emotions. "She brought it up totally unprompted! That should tell you something."

"i bet she could bring it up lol"

"And yet," said Savannah. "How would we know?" FBP shifted his weight to properly angle what was certain to be a devastatingly stupid retort. It was one shift too many. The cabinet gave up the struggle to remain upright and toppled over with a crash. I really should keep better paperwork. Properly chastised, FBP sat in the corner and sulked.

"Have a seat, Savannah," I said, my wits slowly coming back to me like a frightened squirrel who remembered where he stored his nuts. "Care for a drink?"

Savannah glided gracefully across the room and into the chair in front of my desk. I was always jealous of how dames could do that. I wasn't the lightest on my feet – each step for me was another opportunity to hurt myself in a new and exciting way. You would think that, having practiced walking for many years, I would be at least halfway decent at it. You would be wrong.

"I'd love one, Mac," she said. "But I have to make a correction that should answer a few of your questions. I'm Julia. Savannah is my sister."

A twin. I should've known. Actually, wait...strike that. There's no way I could have known that, aside from the fact that an alarming number of my cases seem to involve twins. Something in the water around these parts, I guess. I poured us both a drink. That felt right. I could always count on drink pouring to make sense in this crazy world.

"I see. I'm sorry about your sister," I said, sliding the drink across the desk. "She was a good singer."

"She was a better sister. She died trying to protect me," said Julia. Her hand shook as she lifted the glass to her lips. "I got on the wrong side of some very angry people. I owed them a lot of money."

"What was it, if you don't mind me asking? Drugs? Gambling?"

"Exotic birds."

"what the hell i know girls who are crazy for cock but none who are crazy for cockatoo lol"

"Shut up, FBP," I barked. "Let the lady talk. Sorry about him," I said to Julia. "His brain developed at an inversely proportional rate to his biceps."

"And his biceps are huge," said Savannah.

"Exactly. Now if you don't mind me saying so, miss, as tragic as your situation appears, it seems your problems are over. Someone bumped

FORMER BASEBALL PLAYER SUCKS AT CROWDFUNDING

off your sister thinking she was you, so you're dead to them. I recommend you skip town and try to put this behind you."

"I'm afraid it's not so simple, Mac."

"wait what the hell is going on someone explain this to me is this girl a clone or what lol"

"SHUT UP!" yelled both Julia and I at the same time. We caught each other's eye and she looked away, embarrassed. The good kind of embarrassed where you know she cares what you think. At least a little. I wasn't used to seeing that look. Except at deli counters. I order a lot of meat. And I'm very specific as to its slicing.

"Someone tipped them off that they got the wrong girl. Now my sister's dead and I'm back to where I started," said Julia, her eyes brimming with tears.

"I see. And what exactly would you like me to do about it?" I asked.

"It's the Brunelli Boys that are after me. I was hoping you could convince them to forgive the debt."

"They've already killed once over this debt of yours. And you think I can just talk them out of it?"

"I'm told you can be very...persuasive."

"oh hell yeah does someone need some persuading ill get my persuading stick lol"

"Easy, boy," I said to FBP. "We've gotta find them first. But no offense, miss. I don't know you. What makes this worth my while?"

"I'll see to it that you're very well...compensated," said Julia. The way she

71

looked at me and said the word "compensated" led me to believe that she meant, like, you know. YOU KNOW. Okay, not one of my better descriptions. Words were hard just then.

"Well, I could never turn down a decent compensation," I managed to stammer.

"I've heard that too. I'll try to lay low for a little while. Let you do what you do best," said Julia as she got up and headed for the door. "Oh, and Mac?"

"Yeah?"

"Be careful." She slipped out the door and walked away, her silhouette slowly fading into the distance. I took a deep breath and tried to gather my thoughts. They were like sheep sometimes. And I was a piss-poor shepherd. I poured another drink. Every shepherd needs a crook.

I looked out the window for a minute as my sheep thoughts slowly came back to the pen. Then I grabbed my coat.

"Put some pants on, FBP. I'm serious this time. We're going to see Mabel."

"oh hell no i hate that stupid bitch she can't -"

"Hey, watch your mouth. That's my friend you're talking about. And the best source of information we got. If the Brunelli boys are operating anywhere in the city, she'll know about it. So shut up, get your persuading stick and for the last time, put on some goddamn pants."

We headed out together into the cold, unfeeling city.

FORMER BASEBALL PLAYER SUCKS AT CROWDFUNDING

As the sun set, the fog blew away. Then it realized it didn't have anywhere better to go, came back and really settled in for the long haul.

It took a couple hours to find Mabel. I had to check a few of her normal hangouts before I found her at the corner of North and Wells. Mabel is...how can I put this delicately...a whore. Hmm. There were probably more delicate ways than that. But that's what she was. I'd say she was a hooker with a heart of gold but that's a cliché. Also, it wasn't true. Her heart was bronze at best.

She and I had a bit of a fling a while back. It didn't end well. I ran out of money. She ran out of pity. But we were cordial and she knew everything that happened in the city, so I paid her a visit every now and again. Not like that. Okay, sometimes like that.

I slowly pulled the car up to her corner and rolled the window down. She walked over and leaned in.

"Hey there big boy, you looking for – oh, it's you. And you." Her tired eyes lit up when she saw me. Then darkened again when she saw FBP in the back seat. I made him ride back there ever since an unfortunate wheel-grabbing incident. Now at least when I hear him say, "lets go off-roading lol" it isn't immediately followed by a physical demand to do so. Safer for all involved. Many would worry that this arrangement would make the driver feel like a chauffeur. I feel more like a harried mother with an unruly toddler. Which was worse.

Even on this chilly evening, Mabel wasn't wearing much. But she made what she was wearing count. I caught an eyeful as she leaned in.

"Hey pal," she said sharply. "My eyes are up here."

"I know where your eyes are," I said with a smirk. "I'm looking at your bosoms."

She gave me a hint of a smile. She might as well have been a stablehand for all the bullshit she had to shovel on a daily basis. I think she appreciated my straightforward approach.

"Perv. So what can I do for you?" she said in that low gravelly voice. That voice that sounded like it started from somewhere deep in her chest before being fed through industrial gears like Chaplin in that one movie where he worked in a factory and then finally emerging from her mouth like she barely noticed she was talking. I used to make her read me Chaucer in that voice. She charged extra for that. It was worth it.

"hey baby how much for butt stuff lol"

"There's not enough money in the world, asshole."

"really theres a lot of money in the world put it all together and lets get to business lol"

"Fine, get me the annual GDP of India in rupees and we'll talk."

FORMER BASEBALL PLAYER SUCKS AT CROWDFUNDING

"what the fuck you want to play zelda here i dont think they even have atari yet lol"

Mabel and FBP had only met a couple of times before but she hated him instantly. Most people did, so I suppose that wasn't notable. There was no love lost between the two of them. She hated him like the Royalists hated Oliver Cromwell in 1650. Maybe that's a weird comparison to make, but in 8th grade there was a scheduling mix-up and I had six history classes in one semester. Some of it stuck.

"Sorry about him," I said. "He's a little jumpy."

"yeah id like to be a little jumpy lol jump on you lol i mean jump your bones you get it lol"

We ignored him. "Don't worry about it," said Mabel. "He's probably just mad about his tiny penis."

"Wow, how'd you know?"

"It doesn't take a detective to figure out why some people act the way they do."

She was impressive. Why she ended up in this line of work, I'll never understand. Of course, people probably say the same about me and I don't make nearly as much as her.

"hey baby get out of my dreams and into my car lol"

"First of all, it's not your car," said Mabel.

"Definitely not your car," I echoed.

"Second of all," she continued, "I'd love to get out of your dreams. Consider this a verbal restraining order against your dreams. Finally, you have a tiny penis."

"hey fuck off ive banged hotter chicks than you in my sleep lol"

"Oh, so definitely in your dreams."

"shut...shut up."

I loved watching them verbally spar. It was like watching a boxer get beat up by Godzilla. But I had pressing business, so I couldn't let Godzilla rampage all day.

"Okay, simmer down back there," I said. I tossed him one of those mechanical logic puzzles where two nails are wrapped around each other and you have to twist in just the right way to get them apart. FBP never managed to solve them, but violently bending the nails would keep him occupied for a while.

"I'm here on business, Mabel. Need some information."

"Oh, just business? That's a shame." The look in her eyes made my head swim. I tried to calm down. I often had to tell myself it could never happen between us. Our relationship was like my 8th grade class schedule: too much history.

"Yeah, just business. Got a client who's in deep in exotic bird debt to the Brunelli boys. Need to talk them into forgiveness. Or at least a sensible payment plan. Know where I can find them?"

Her eyes narrowed as she stood up with a start. She looked around like she was trying to remember where she put her keys, then leaned back in.

"You say the Brunelli boys?"

FORMER BASEBALL PLAYER SUCKS AT CROWDFUNDING

"Yeah. There a problem?"

"Maybe. Let me check on a couple things. Meet me at Belmont Harbor in an hour. And as much as I hate to say it, bring the big guy. I think you're getting played."

"Played? What the hell are you talking about, Mabel?"

"I'll explain later. One hour, okay Mac?"

"Sure. Hey Mabel," I said as she started to walk away.

"Yeah?"

"Be safe."

"Never," she said with a smile and then disappeared into the night.

I sighed. "These broads are gonna be the death of me," I said.

"solved it lol" FBP held up two bent and separated nails in his bleeding hands.

"Nice job, buddy," I said as I started to drive off. "Let's go get a drink, whaddya say?"

The fog tried to remember something from its fog childhood, but the memory was...foggy.

It was an hour and a half later when FBP and I made our way toward Belmont Harbor. Just like money and my gun, I often lost track of time. As we got close, we could hear the distinct sound of two female voices arguing. That was a rarity for me. I was more used to holding up one half of that equation.

We stayed out of sight until we were close enough to make out what they were saying. I crouched down to hide behind a shipping crate. I motioned for FBP to do the same but instead he walked right into a forklift. Close enough.

I peeked out from the side of the crate and saw the unmistakable form of Mabel, but the other girl was standing right behind her. I couldn't make out who it was until the argument grew heated enough that a shift in physical position was warranted. Mabel angrily stepped to the side to reveal a furious Julia.

"what the fuck is going on what is she doing here"

I hated how much we were agreeing today.

"are they gonna make out oh yeah baby things are heating up lol"

I wished that was the case. I even allowed myself a couple seconds of imagining it. But from the looks of things, that dream wasn't going to be coming true tonight.

"You stupid bitch," snarled Mabel. "You owe <u>me</u> money for those damn exotic birds. The Brunelli boys haven't been in the bird business for years. What the hell are you doing putting Mac on their tail?"

"He was investigating my sister's murder, you dumb whore!" Julia put a point on the word "whore" that made it clear that she wasn't using it in the affectionate way that sorority girls did. "I had to throw him off the trail. Besides, the Brunelli boys are assholes. Getting them roughed up would be icing on the cake."

Wait, this wasn't making any sense. Why would Julia want to throw me off the trail of her sister's murderer?

FORMER BASEBALL PLAYER SUCKS AT CROWDFUNDING

"Wait," said Mabel. "That doesn't make any sense. Why would you want to throw Mac off the trail of your sister's murderer?"

Oh. Good. I could stay behind the crate for a little while longer.

"Oh, it's already been solved. I did it," said Julia proudly.

Holy shit. On the one hand, this case just got a lot easier. On the other hand, getting fairly compensated just got a lot harder.

"Jesus," said Mabel, noticeably shaken. "Why the hell would you kill your sister?"

"Because...she was always prettier than me."

"You're TWINS!!"

Okay. Now was as good a time as any to make my entrance. "Ladies ladies, let's all calm down," is what I planned to say as I stepped out from behind my hiding place. I got as far as the "la." That's when Julia pulled the gun out of her purse and I ducked right the hell back before she could see me.

"This ends now," said Julia coldly. She pointed the gun right at Mabel. "I should have done this a long time ago. Of course, it's not as clean as the icicle I used on my sister, but it'll have to do."

You've got to be fucking kidding me. She actually used an icicle. I didn't know which way was up anymore.

"And besides, who's going to miss one ugly little whore?" said Julia, cocking the gun.

That snapped me back to my senses. I was out of time. "Okay, FBP! Get her!" I whispered.

He jumped out and without a moment's thought walked right up to Mabel and snapped her neck with his bare hands.

Shit. Should've been more specific. That one's on me.

"Okay, that one's on me, pal! I meant the other one! The one with the gun! Get her!"

He charged Julia like an angry rhinoceros. Like a double-horned Sumatran rhinoceros that had been incorrectly referred to as a single-horned Indian variety. They hate that. Makes 'em real angry. He charged like one of those.

She got off a wild shot in sheer panic. It whizzed right by his crotch. Good thing he had such a tiny penis or else it would have been shot right off. He was on her in three steps and then she was gone. All was quiet except for the sounds of the water lapping against the dock.

I ran up to Mabel and cradled her head in my hands. I could almost hear that beautiful voice of hers telling me what an idiot I was. "Yeah, sorry about that," I said softly. "Not my best work. Maybe your next life will be better anyway. I hope we meet again." I'm a Buddhist. Didn't seem appropriate to mention until now. I could hear sirens faintly off in the distance, but I didn't care. I just knelt there, smoothing Mabel's hair.

"hey two dead chicks and the cops are coming cheeze it the fuzz you know lol"

FORMER BASEBALL PLAYER SUCKS AT CROWDFUNDING

"Hey, FBP?"

"yeah"

"You're a fucking idiot."

"hey fuck you too man im outta here lol"

I started to see the lights from the police cars. Red blue red blue red blue. It made the whole scene look like a shitty dance club. FBP stepped behind a crate and there was a flash of blue. It could've been from the cars but I didn't know. I didn't know anything anymore. Wait...I did know one thing. I shouldn't be here right now.

"Hey, FBP! You're right, pal. We gotta get outta here. FBP!"

He was gone.

Shit. This one was going to be tough to explain. The sirens grew closer.

The fog just fogged all over the place without a care in the goddamn world.

DAN RYCKERT AND FRIENDS

FORMER BASEBALL PLAYER SUCKS AT CROWDFUNDING

Chapter Seven

By Jason Berger (@jayberger)

The Year 2001

    The water felt cool on his face. At 6:40am it was still early - too early - for him to be awake but today there was a reason; a mission.

    He realized the water was cool, COLD even. Cold water was a luxury - no one in this airport restroom realizes it. No one is as - is it grateful? Yes. He felt something. He was awakened by the splash of cold. He pumped the soap twice into the palm of his hand, switched the handle to H - *hot*, another luxury, and he thought long and hard about what was about to happen.

    Mohamed Atta had spent the better part of two years in America learning how to fly a plane in Florida, and laying low. It was surprisingly easy since this country was so confident and unaware of what he could do; *will do*. He came here with a true hate of this country, this country's laws, this country's gluttony, this country's religious beliefs. He had spent two years with same daily routine, planning for today. A day that if he went through with it would change the world. He would be dead, charred and ash. He would be remembered as a soldier by a small amount of people, someone who just did what he was told, and he would be forcefully forgotten by everyone else in the world. <u>That</u> is the power he held in the form of a makeshift knife in this pocket of his GAP shirt. A shirt he chose because it made him blend in with the rest of the American population, a sensible shirt that fit nice and didn't cost a lot of money. He looked at his reflection in the mirror and saw someone that over the course of two years had changed from the man he was when he entered this country.

He thought for a second - what if I just walk out of this airport? What if I just walked away? Got in a cab, went to a McDonald's and had an Egg McMuffin and a cup of coffee like so many Americans were doing right now. Being normal, going about their lives happily or unhappily but feeling something. What if I did that? The others would go about their mission and most likely follow through with it, but if I didn't it would throw everything off.

A man walked up next to him. "Mornin'" he said and began to wash his hands. Cordial. A human being respecting a stranger's existence for no reason other than to acknowledge that he is another person simply sharing the same

FORMER BASEBALL PLAYER SUCKS AT CROWDFUNDING

public sink that he is. This man didn't have to say anything, he could wash his hands and walk away never to be seen or heard from again, but this man made a choice to say something because this person *had made a choice to be nice*; to be good. Mohamed broke a small, ineffective smile and slight nod of the head to acknowledge the man's genuine greeting. The man pulled two sheets of hand towels - HAND TOWELS! A luxury! - wiped his hands dry, balled up the towels and lobbed them at the trashcan. He missed. "Aw, shucks. Woulda been three points! Ha!" Instead of leaving the garbage on the ground, the man picked up the towels and dropped them into the trash. "Have a good day," he said and walked out, ready to board a plane and return to his home, his family, his dog, his car, his CD collection, his books, his barbeque grill, his bank account, his LIFE.

Mohamed Atta checked his watch. 6:45am. The flight was about to board and he would change the country for many years. But after seeing this man, a man he would've had murdered and beheaded if this were his country, he felt something different. He didn't wish to go through with the plan.

Mohamed walked over to the bank of ten urinals. Urinals, a designated place to urinate, unlike back in his home country where men just urinated wherever they felt, and women were beheaded if they did within sight of man, or the much holier, goat. He had come to understand the "rules" of urinating in public. These urinals had no divider between them so he walked towards the end of the bank and used the one closest to the wall. He didn't know why he did this, but he did it because he learned it from Americans. No one else was in the bathroom at the time. He didn't have to urinate, but stood there thinking he might as well get everything out now.

Then a man walked in.

More ego than man, in fact. He was wearing Oakley razor blade sunglasses, a visor, and a Hooters tank top tucked into Zubaz shorts. He walked over to the urinal right next to Mohamed and unzipped his pants. No one else was in the restroom at the time. Why this Ego decided to choose this particular urinal didn't make sense to Mohamed. There were eight other urinals! The man began to urinate which immediately made any chance of Mohamed urinating a memory. The Ego began to whistle a song, Limp Bizkit's *'Rollin''* and looked over at Mohamed.

"That's a pretty nice dick...for a baby. You have a baby dick, bro."

FORMER BASEBALL PLAYER SUCKS AT CROWDFUNDING

Mohamed felt shame. He looked over at The Ego's penis, much smaller than his own, but Mohamed would not say anything because it felt impolite, yet another virtue he had learned from his two years in the "Home Of The Free". Mohamed pretended to finish urinating and walked back over to the sink. The Ego's stream was so loud he almost congratulated himself on such a powerful expulsion with a confident smile. The stream stopped.

"Houston, we have a problem!" said The Ego. And then punctuated the sentence with an incredibly loud, muffled flatulence. At which point the urination stream continued.

Another man walked into the restroom. He immediately recognized The Ego and said something to the effect of "Holy shit, you're…" Mohamed didn't hear the last part as he had turned on the sink to wash his hands again. Something he now felt was meditative.

"Yo, can I have your autograph?" the man asked, new to the restroom.

"Sure!" said The Ego.

The Ego then turned and urinated at the man's feet.

"Aw what the fuck, dude?" said the man. "I don't do autographs. You people just try and sell them for $6 dollars and then spend that money on whatever the fuck shitheads buy for

$6. Now you have a story, and that's priceless. Plus, you can tell people I called you a gay."

"You didn't call me a..."

"You're a gay," said The Ego, smiling.

"I walked right into that. That's on me." the man said.

The man was visibly angry, as would anyone who was just urinated upon. He stormed out of the restroom leaving Mohamed alone again with The Ego.

Mohamed closed his eyes and rubbed his hands under the warm water. It soothed him. He had just made a decision, on his own, for the first time in his life. He will leave the airport and find a new life, a new name, he will keep his beliefs but adjust to the more "liberal" sect of his religion. He will buy a house, and a car. He will buy into this "American Dream" he was sent here to rage against. This Ego that was in the bathroom with him was not representative of all Americans, yet he WAS representative of what Mohamed hated about Americans when he came over.

"How you doin', dipshit?" The Ego said. Mohamed said nothing, continuing to rub his hands hands together under the soothing warm water.

"Hey dummy, I'm talking to you." The Ego would be relentless about starting a conversation

FORMER BASEBALL PLAYER SUCKS AT CROWDFUNDING

with Mohamed, so Mohamed did what he learned was a polite, human acknowledgement: He smiled and nodded.

The Ego took that as a challenge, as would most douchebag, no-dick wannabe Alpha males that only think of themselves and no one else. Unfortunately for Mohamed Atta, he didn't know to just continue to ignore someone provoking him. He had been in America for some time, but "sincerity as sarcasm" was a mask he could not wear.

The Ego grabbed Mohamed by the collar of his GAP shirt and lifted him up. The man WAS strong. Because of steroids his arms grew as large as his balls shrunk small. Mohamed was frightened. Nervous. He just wanted to leave and go start a life, but this dumb hulk wouldn't let him go. And why? Why would a stranger just do this?

"Get the fuck out of America, Shit-for-Skin." said The Ego before launching Mohamed into the trash can. A pile of hand towels, boarding passes, and McDonald's bags all spilled out. Mohamed laid in the things that Americans were spoiled with. He laid in their trash, he *felt* like their trash.

"I'm just fucking with you." The Ego threw a hundred dollar at Mohamed and casually exited the restroom. A moment later, a flash of light and an otherworldly sound came from outside.

Mohamed stood up, walked to the mirror, turned on the sink to wash the tobacco spit from a discarded Snapple bottle that broke when he landed off his hands.

The water was neither warm nor cold.

Mohamed felt nothing anymore, rage, pain, embarrassment, all checked in from their lunch break inside his head. Mohamed was there to complete a mission he was called to do. For a moment he got side-tracked, thinking that Americans were kind souls. The kind gesture by the man from earlier was no longer a memory, but a taunt to bring about fear into the American world. The Ego woke up a sleeping lion inside Mohamed, and as he walked out of the restroom and onto the plane, he only hoped that The Ego would realize that the destruction that will be birthed that day. The fear, the paranoia, the broken families, the newly formed overprotective, cautious American life from that moment forward was his fault. All because The Ego was a big 'ol stinky piece of farty shit.

FORMER BASEBALL PLAYER SUCKS AT CROWDFUNDING

Chapter Eight

By Dave Hinkle (@DaveHinkle)

The Year 2002

The portal opened silently, dumping Former Baseball Player onto the sidewalk with enough force that he took a good five-foot bounce, gracefully landing on all fours like a cat. Rampant steroid abuse had its perks, include dense, rubbery muscles and cat-like safety mechanisms.

FBP then rose to all fours and jammed a needle into his butt. The steroids rushed into his cheek as he wiped his hands on his baseball pants. The pants, quite tight, weren't the most flattering. Former Baseball Player had the kind of micro-penis that could split a pistachio nut. God had truly cursed him.

The alley he found himself in was instantly recognizable. The sticky heat of the Miami night clung to his face, neck, chest, and crotch, pooling in a moist river at the base of his smooth Ken doll groin. Unfortunately, he had found that the moisture had no plumping effect on his micro-penis.

In the alley, FBP jammed another needle into his ass and noticed a neon sign for The Miami Musclehead, his favorite bar and steroid-copping grounds from his baseball days. This was a Miami dude's bar, through and through, where the pina coladas flowed and the dudes cut the mid-drift from their shirts. These were well-bronzed Miami badasses, the kind of dudes who could really recommend a great taco place with the perfect bathroom to shoot steroids up in.

FBP, a regular at the club during his heyday, strolled up to the back door and injected himself again. He walked in and was met by a bouncer who instantly recognized him and gave him the nod to go on in. In the span of 15 minutes, FBP noticed a lively mix of Shaggy, Nickelback, O-Town and Blu Cantrell. Clearly whomever had set up this sweet mix on the jukebox had only the finest taste in early 2000s music.

Across the dance floor, he noticed his brother Other Former Baseball Player stroll in through the front door. His brother was not only gifted by a penis many women have said "exists" in contrast to his own, FBP's brother also had a much better sense of style than FBP. He wore sunglasses indoors with neon-green and pink Zubaz pants, a fishnet muscle shirt and a leather jacket, which came together to give Other Former Baseball Player a commanding presence.

As Other Former Baseball Player entered the club, high-fiving his imaginary friends and awkwardly grinding on groups of disinterested women, FBP moved through the crowd to meet him. "Brother!" FBP screamed over Lifehouse's "Hanging by a Moment."

Other Former Baseball Player cooly pulled his sunglasses down over the edge of his nose

FORMER BASEBALL PLAYER SUCKS AT CROWDFUNDING

and shot FBP a glance. A wide grin slowly opened above his thick, bulbous chin. "Brother!" The two high-fived and shared a shot of creatine that Other Former Baseball Player hid in his leather jacket's inside pocket for special occasions.

As the creatine took over, the two engaged in a push-up contest on the dance floor. They could feel their muscles clench and lungs burn. Just as both brothers were getting into that euphoric zone of pump nirvana, The Beach Boys suddenly came on.

The two brothers froze, angered by the fact a California band would get playtime on a Miami jukebox. The only thing people in Miami hated more than carbs were California – and anything having to do with that wretched state.

Both brothers looked over to the jukebox and that's when they saw them: two muscular blonde gentlemen, wearing matching grey tanktops with the California state flag proudly on display. The two men, tourists in town for a dumbbell convention, wanted to test their mettle against all Miami had to offer. Where better to represent Cali muscle than at The Miami Musclehead?

The larger of the two ripped the jukebox off the wall without a grimace and smashed it on the ground. His name was Taylor and his smaller, more mouthy friend was Cody. The two had met at Venice Beach and been pumping together ever since.

"Push-ups? Like, really? Is that, like, how

things are done here in Miami? Pathetic. In California, we do burpees – like a totally much more difficult exercise." Cody spoke with alacrity and precision that the Player brothers found difficult to keep up with. FBP himself had only just cracked the crossword puzzle on the back of the Honey Golden Grahams box. 14 down, crunchitude, stumped him for a good month.

At this point, three minutes had gone by and neither Player brother had said a thing. In fact, FBP had already walked away, distracted by a strobe light. The blondes, out of sheer boredom, then turned to walk away.

"Miami good, California bad!" Other Former Baseball Player was proud of how many words he strung together in his sick burn. His timing left a little to be desired.

"It speaks! Well, like, we'll have to do something about that." Cody motioned to Taylor, who produced a glossy 8X10 of five-time Mr. Universe bodybuilding champion, Bill Pearl. Bill was a legend to everyone from the Pacific Northwest, having risen to relevance on the world stage – an almost impossible feat coming from somewhere so plain and boring as the Pacific Northwest – by taking way more steroids than anybody else at the time. Doing that took *real* guts and everyone from the PNW knew that.

Taylor ripped the picture in half and let it drop to the ground. Other Former Baseball Player dropped to his knees, gasping for breath and clutching at his exposed mid-drift in pain.

FORMER BASEBALL PLAYER SUCKS AT CROWDFUNDING

Turns out a good base tan does nothing to dull the pain of watching two dicks desecrate a Pacific Northwest legend.

Cody kneeled down besides Other Former Baseball Player and pulled out a piece of paper from the pocket of his sweat shorts. It was a deed for The Miami Musclehead.

"That's right, the place is, like, ours. We're totally bringing California and its world-class excellence in bodybuilding to this disgusting little swamp state. We're, like, taking over. Soon, all of these precious plastic surgeons and Cuban coffee places will be replaced by cool California plastic surgeons and Starbucks."

FBP was still over in the corner, staring at that strobe light.

"No! Me no like that!" Other Former Baseball Player could barely spit out the words – half because he was still catching his breath and half because he, like his brother, was borderline mentally retarded.

"We make contest!" The line was a last-ditch effort to try and save the club. By challenging these California hunks, who were clearly more intelligent and successful than Other Former Baseball Player and his occupied brother, Other Former Baseball Player was finding it harder and harder to lie to himself with each passing moment. No matter what contest he thought up, he would be no match for these two.

"I do believe he, like, wants to challenge us for the club, Taylor," Cody cackled at his brother. "This is going to be like totally great. Name the event – if we win, you have to leave in shame, totally nude, and if you win, you can save the club. Do you understand?"

Other Former Baseball Player was drooling a bit now. Those were a lot of words and his brain was working in overdrive. In an exaggerated, totally cartoonish way, he jerked his head up and down.

FBP was still staring at the strobe light, unaware of what was going on. At some point, he decided to remove his pants.

"We'll even give you the advantage: push-ups. Whoever can do the most push-ups, you or my friend Taylor here, wins. Go!"

Other Former Baseball Player dropped to the ground like a bag full of steroids. Taylor slowly and gracefully dropped to his stomach. The two began counting off. One. Two. Three.

The two quickly found their stride. They thrusted their bodies from the floor to the sky with consistent, powerful force. Their rippling muscles, the result of years of steroid abuse, parted the air molecules and caused a burning friction that set the roof of the Miami Musclehead ablaze.

Four hundred. Four hundred and one. Four hundred and two.

Cody, standing above both participants, laughed maniacally as the building burned. Most of the other patrons in The Miami Musclehead barely noticed what was going on. They were far too busy comparing their delts and drinking their

FORMER BASEBALL PLAYER SUCKS AT CROWDFUNDING

pina coladas.

Seven thousand four hundred and eight. Seven thousand four hundred and nine. Seven thousand four-ten.

Neither refused to give up. Neither would let the other win. Both men were fiercely determined and yet both men felt a sick pain in the pit of their stomachs.

The two had clearly not injected steroids into their buttholes for at least an hour. To put it in terms a steroid-free person could understand, it's like spending a year roaming the desert without a drop of steroids. For a roided-out freak, that's an unacceptable existence.

One hundred and eighty-two thousand and four. One hundred and eighty-two thousand and five. One hundred and eighty-two thousand and six.

They say that twins have an unspoken connection. This is true – if one twin scrapes a knee, the other twin will feel a phantom pain. The dull ache of muscles yearning for go-juice was the only thing powerful enough to rip FBP away from the strobe light. But because FBP's mental level was just below that of an old discarded carton of milk, he understood the pain to be his own.

His inability to read clocks only reinforced the idea that FBP had felt like he hadn't taken steroids in a while, even though he shot up like four times before he even walked into The Miami Musclehead. So FBP made a bee-line for the bathroom.

FBP headed into the first open stall, refusing to make eye contact with the bathroom attendant. FBP was the kind of guy who never washed his hands after using the bathroom – both one and two. He always felt like germs were the best way to give your immune system a pump, even though he never fully understood what an immune system was.

He slowly pulled the needle out of his carrying case and filled its plastic tube with a healthy dose of steroids. This part was always FBP's favorite part of the ritual, when his micro-penis would feel the rush of a micrometer of blood. It was the only way he could get a hard-on.

As he pushed the plunger down, he felt his acne-riddled buttcheek tighten from the rush of steroids. The steroids acting as a rejuvenating cocktail of strength and confidence most men would simply look to their adequate penises for. Since Former Baseball Player was without an adequate penis – in fact, to the naked eye, his penis was invisible. That's truly how small FBP's penis was.

But that didn't matter right now. The steroids were kicking in and FBP's hot Cuban blood began to boil. FBP needed someone to hurt; he needed something to focus his rage on. He kicked open the stall door and stomped out of the bathroom.

Two million one hundred and eighteen thousand, four hundred and four. Two million one hundred and eighteen thousand, four

FORMER BASEBALL PLAYER SUCKS AT CROWDFUNDING

hundred and five. Two million one hundred and eighteen thousand, four hundred and six.

"Hahahaha I can, like, totally see you slowing down, you filthy Miami-loving trash!" Cody, moving through a series of more progressively intricate poses that showcased his perfect muscle definition, never saw the punch coming. FBP connected with a haymaker right on Cody's nose, breaking it instantly. Cody dropped to the ground as blood gushed from his nasal cavity, soaking his tiny grey tanktop immediately.

Taylor, slightly winded from doing a moderate amount of push-ups, jumped to his feet in disbelief. "Dude you, like, totally punched him. Not cool, bro."

FBP had already grabbed a bar stool and was mid-swing when Taylor finished his sentence. The stool connected with Taylor's mouth. His lip took most of the damage and was completely slashed open, spilling blood all over the rich lacquer of the dance floor.

FBP stood atop the blondes, victorious, and shot some more steroids into his butthole. Other Former Baseball Player continued to do push-ups since nobody told him to stop. He was nearing one billion at this point.

That's when the police, led by police chief John F. Timoney, came piling into the club.

"You've done the city of Miami a great service today, boys. You warded off any other potential tourists considering spending time in Miami – and you did it with completely unwarranted violence. You have made Miami proud."

At this point, FBP completely forgot where he was and started to look over toward the strobe light again.

"Former Baseball Player and Other Former Baseball Player," Timoney said, catching FBP's attention once more, "the city of Miami thanks you. Johnson, Mahoney – cuff these Cali boys and get 'em processed."

The cops lifted the defeated blondes and escorted them out of The Miami Musclehead. Timoney, impressed with the speed and brutality of FBP's unnecessary assault on two relatively innocent tourists from California, then shook the boys' hands and fired a few rounds of his pistol off into the air. After standing around for about three minutes in silence, shooting glances at both Player brothers while waiting for some kind of response, Timoney awkwardly turned around and walked out the front door.

The two brothers, high on the rush of victory, then began competing against each other. FBP removed his shirt and flexed his pecs, which caused Other Former Baseball Player to take off his leather jacket and fishnet shirt and flex his back muscles. Other Former Baseball Player then ripped off his Zubaz pants to show off his powerful thighs. FBP removed his unflattering baseball slacks and started to do squats in place.

Then, in the heat of the moment, Other Former Baseball Player ripped off his underwear

FORMER BASEBALL PLAYER SUCKS AT CROWDFUNDING

and went completely nude. He had one thing to flex that FBP didn't: a completely average and wholly unimpressive penis.

FBP was scared to expose his largely invisible member to a club full of his kin. Former Baseball Player's tiny, minuscule penis, desperate to keep its existence a secret from the world, compelled him to back down. In response, FBP jammed another needle full of steroids into his butt.

The steroids, keen on dominating the competition and further spreading acne across FBP's back and butt, wouldn't let him back down. It was just like the plot to his favorite movie, *She's All That.*

"No, I make better good muscle!" FBP screamed at the top of his lungs and ripped his underwear off. That's when the room fell silent.

Everyone thought they were looking at a dickless freak, but in reality they were looking at a guy whose dick is so small, it's imperceptible to the human eye. FBP's penis was so small that even if a women had allowed him to penetrate her, his penis would only touch air.

Former Baseball Player's dick is tiny.

Everyone was laughing now, even FBP's brother. Despite all of his success as a baseball player, Former Baseball Player could never fill a vagina. He would never be able to pleasure a woman in the way any other man on the planet Earth could. His dick was truly tiny.

And it was this revelation that taught him the secret to happiness: If you have a tiny penis, be an asshole to people, shoot up steroids all the time and solve all your problems with violence. Punch the penis pain away and find serenity.

It was certainly a way to explain FBP's penchant for violence and why he absolutely loved Porsche convertibles. With this wisdom, he could still carve out an identity for himself that wasn't predicated upon having a penis. Well, a penis anyone could see, anyway.

Of course, in his mind, it wasn't such an eloquent thought. It was mainly a garbled mess of red flashes and confusing letter shapes. But still, for Former Baseball Player, it was a breakthrough.

FBP then punched his brother in the face, knocking him out cold. FBP gathered his brother's clothes and began to dress himself. 32 minutes later, he was dressed.

FBP celebrated successfully dressing himself without assistance by injecting a shot of steroids. As the chemicals started to take effect, FBP felt a small tinge of regret for punching his brother. Assaulting strangers was one thing, but did his brother deserve his wrath?

"Him penis have," FBP grunted out, as if he was asked a question by some ghost in the room. At this point, nobody even knew he was in the room. As if on cue, a portal silently opened on the dance floor.

The portal looked like one big strobe light and with that, FBP started to walk toward it. The closer he got, the more tumescent his micro-dong became at the prospect of new people to

FORMER BASEBALL PLAYER SUCKS AT CROWDFUNDING

assault. His mind raced at the possibility of ignorantly whomping on more innocent people. With a vacant look in his eyes and a healthy sum of drool accumulating in his mouth, Former Baseball Player walked through the portal.

DAN RYCKERT AND FRIENDS

FORMER BASEBALL PLAYER SUCKS AT CROWDFUNDING

Chapter Nine

By Dave Rudden (@DaveRudden)

The Year 1994

Former Baseball Player popped out of the portal at the gates of a palatial estate in a fancy Southern California suburb, one that looked a lot like Brentwood, but there was no way of telling, really. He picked up a newspaper at his feet that showed the date June 12, 1994. Fortunately, Former Baseball Player was pretty sure he wouldn't run into himself, because if he was playing baseball back then, his team wasn't in California that day.

He could see the mailbox by the door. It read "Former Football Player and Family." Former Baseball Player claimed to love football, since it's the most American sport there is and a favorite pastime in the Pacific Northwest (which is very far away from Cuba). He forgot about his time-travel ordeal for a moment and decided he'd ask for Former Football Player's advice in breaking into pro football, since baseball players that people actually admire (like Bo Jackson and Deion Sanders) managed to juggle baseball and football careers, while Former Baseball Player had to basically freebase steroids to get ahead in his career.

He was able to clear the barb-wire fence (the crotch of his baseball pants caught on the wire, but he didn't suffer any injury due to the large distance between the fabric of the pants and the tip of his very small penis), landing next to a guest house. He peeked inside and saw a very untalented actor, the kind of guy who would use the fallout from a murder trial to milk 15 minutes of fame. "This guy's obviously not a football player," Former Baseball Player thought. "He's obviously not abusing steroids like I am."

Former Baseball Player proceeded further towards the mansion, stopping in his tracks momentarily when he heard a man and woman screaming. The door busted open, with a large (and very panicked) man covered in blood. He caught Former Baseball Player in his gaze, and became even more worried. "Look..." the man said. "I can explain..."

"Former Football Player?!" Former Baseball Player said. "Name's Former Baseball Player! I'm a huge fan!" He ran up and shook Former Football Player's hands. They were covered with wet gloves, the kind that would shrink if left to dry with the blood of two innocent people. Former Football Player smirked, realizing that the man in front of him was oblivious to what had just happened.

"Gee, Former Football Player," Former Baseball Player said "I'd really like it if you could impart some tips so I could play professional football. I'm totally willing to take more steroids if

FORMER BASEBALL PLAYER SUCKS AT CROWDFUNDING

possible. In return, I can give you baseball tips, and help you break into the majors!"

"Nah, that won't be necessary where I'm going..." Former Football Player said. "But perhaps you can help me with other things." He walked with Former Baseball Player over to an area where the bloodied, unmoving bodies of a man and woman lay. Former Baseball Player had a quizzical look on his face, but before he could say something, Former Football Player interjected "Tip number one! Find good training partners! These two are just tuckered out... we all had a really intense scrimmage game earlier. So, uh... why don't we clean up and let these two rest?"

Former Baseball Player grabbed a rag and started wiping away some of the blood staining the driveway. He got some near Former Football Player's Ford Bronco and elsewhere, really just spreading the blood around rather than cleaning anything up. "Well, he did an awful job of actually cleaning the area," Former Football Player thought. "But perhaps the extra DNA around here will cause the local police to really fuck up investigating this murder scene."

"Alright, Former Baseball Player," Former Football Player said. "In order to truly become a pro football player, you need to dress like one. So, uh, why don't you wear my shoes and socks for a bit." Most people would be suspicious of such a request, but Former Baseball Player was dumb enough to think nothing of it, so he traipsed around in Former Football Player's footwear for a while. Despite being covered with blood, Former Baseball Player was still impressed with the quality of the shoes, which were probably made by some fancy footwear maker like Bruno Magli. After spending enough time in a probable murderer's shoes, Former Baseball Player gave them back, eagerly awaiting the next tip.

"Tip number three is a big one." Former Football Player said. "You have to know the right people. Here's a number for a sports agent, and I bet he could give you your big break in pro football. Go into the den and give this guy a call. I'll give you some privacy."

Former Baseball Player walked through the mansion, noting the movie posters featuring Former Football Player. He was in a comedy series, the first of which was a classic, but the next two in the franchise were kind of overkill. He passed some of Former Football Player's old football gear set aside to be shipped to a Vegas sports memorabilia dealer, who had purchased them legally. He picked up the phone and dialed the number.

Before Former Baseball Player could say anything, the man on the other side of the line said. "LAPD, how can I... wait a second, I know this number! This is Former Football Player! You're a different race from me! I'm going to head over right now and mess your place up something proper!"

Former Baseball Player was panicked. He tried calling 911 to report the problem, but he

FORMER BASEBALL PLAYER SUCKS AT CROWDFUNDING

ended up ordering even more police to come. With the situation getting more chaotic by the minute, he sprinted outside. "Former Football Player!" he yelled, distracting Former Football Player from his knife-cleaning efforts. "I think I got a wrong number. Some racist cop is going to head over here right now!"

"Oh dear..." Former Football Player said in a tone so facetious that anyone with more brain cells than Former Baseball Player would have noticed. "We should get out of here. I don't want to run into that guy, so I'm going to hop over the back fence. I've got a pretty small penis, so I don't have to worry about catching my groin on the barb wire. You should come back the way you came."

Former Baseball Player thought of commenting on and bonding about their similarly-small shlongs, but he wanted to escape before the police arrived. He again climbed the gate, avoiding cuts to his almost-inverted penis and admired Former Football Player as he sprinted in the opposite direction. "Truly, that is one of history's greatest men."

Former Baseball Player spotted a cavalcade of cop cars arriving on the scene. "Oh dear..." Former Baseball Player said. "That's too many cops for this house. I bet they disturb those two sleeping scrimmage players and track blood from the practice everywhere."

Former Baseball Player had but a moment to make his escape before the racist cop and his coworkers arrived. He hopped off the fence, but before he could hit the ground, another portal swallowed him whole.

FORMER BASEBALL PLAYER SUCKS AT CROWDFUNDING

Chapter Ten

By Brandon Stroud (@MrBrandonStroud)

The Year 3030

Boy's first memory in his short, endless life was of a baseball field in mid-September. He'd been on the planet for a few weeks now, and though his brain wouldn't let him remember the names of the players or the numbers on the scoreboard, it wouldn't let him forget the smell of freshly-cut grass, the crisp whiff of a bat missing a change-up or the sea of empty green chairs that seemed to stretch off in every direction for miles and miles. He remembered his newborn fingers stretching and grasping for his mother's breast, and how she'd paid like eight dollars for a pretzel that wasn't even good. It was hard, and she had no place to put mustard. He wasn't sure why he remembered that.

The rest he pieced together from conjecture and tall tales told by his camp elders as they slowly died from radiation poisoning. The game wasn't even over when the bombs fell. Boy's mother had collapsed down a flight of steps and used her last, living breath to hide the infant in the decapitated head of an anthropomorphic plush elephant. It had protected him from the brunt of the blast while the stadium rotted away from the inside and collapsed, taking almost 400 fans down with it. Nearly a month later, a survivalist caravan moved through the area and discovered him alive and well, still inside the mascot head, still trying to bite through a rigid log of inedible pretzel.

Ten years had passed, and the war began.

Boy shuffled his feet quietly along the ashen, dusty trail, the rumbling of his stomach echoing through his body. He hadn't eaten for days. His last meal had been the scraps of a post-apocalyptic strip club buffet he'd been given by Former Baseball Player, a hard, enormous man who'd taken custody of him in the wilds of New America because he couldn't convince any of the rabid dogs he'd found to follow him through the wasteland. Former Baseball Player had emerged from a portal three months ago, six-foot-four and full of muscles, with beautiful blue contact lenses and jet black hair slicked back against his blaze orange scalp. They'd been traveling together, united by two common goals: reaching the independent city-state of Oak Land, and survival. Boy's heart couldn't keep him alive on a memory, and he needed to retrace his steps back to those sounds and seats where it had all began. Oak Land is also where Former Baseball Player kept a lot of his stuff.

Boy was dying -- he knew this -- but he still looked upon Former Baseball Player with admiration. The man's natural strength and speed were enough to excuse how much of an asshole he was to everyone. Relationships in New America were known to form quickly and end suddenly, so beggars couldn't be choosers, as it

FORMER BASEBALL PLAYER SUCKS AT CROWDFUNDING

were. Maybe he'd rather be crossing the wasteland with Bo Jackson, but this was still pretty good. Former Baseball Player had never had children, at least not any children he cared about, and he took guardianship of Boy very seriously. "I'd do anything for this kid," he thought to himself. "Except sign an autograph."

"Shh," Former Baseball Player gestured suddenly. Boy's eyes raised and darted, taking in the grey Earth, grey trees and constantly-falling grey ashes. "Over there," Former continued.

That's when Boy saw it. A turned-over semi truck with the word FOOD written across it in big letters. He couldn't believe it...the vehicle was in mint condition, aside from the whole "being turned over on its side" thing, and the cargo doors were still tightly sealed. They were the first to find it. Not the soulless, brainless overlord Commissioner. Not the savage, loincloth-wearing for some reason, tomahawk and crossbow-carrying for some reason Rangers.

"What could be inside?" Boy asked.

"Probably food, you little dipshit," Former responded.

Boy crouched and watched quietly as Former Baseball Player leapt the grey, ashy brush and crept toward the truck. His stomach let out a loud growl, causing Former to turn back to him and mouth, "the fuck are you doing, shut up, seriously." Boy mouthed back, "sorry," and clutched his sunken belly, praying for its silence. Former looked around for a few seconds, and upon determining the mile-or-so radius around the truck to be completely empty, unsheathed his club-like walking stick and began hacking wildly at the truck's locks. He was strong and surprisingly accurate with his strikes, but he didn't seem to care about what he was doing so it took him way longer than expected.

Finally, with one (okay, four) strong swings, Former cracked the lock and the truck's door popped open. With a cocky grin, Former flung open the door and revealed the truck's contents: stacks and stacks of cardboard boxes with STEROIDS written on them in Sharpie. "Jackpot," Former Baseball Player scoffed.

As Former climbed into the back, Boy pushed his way through the dead branches and scurried up to claim his share. By the time he reached the truck, Former was already standing and wrapping his arms around as many boxes as possible.

"No, these are mine," Former barked.

"Are they food?"

"For me they are," he boasted. "You don't get to have any until I'm done. If you eat before I tell you to, I'll write down BOY DID STEROIDS in my journal and give it to the Commissioner. Then he'll know that you broke into the truck and stole somebody else's stuff. You wouldn't want that, would you? Shut up, don't answer me, I know I'm right."

Boy knew Former Baseball Player was right. That night, the two set up camp outside of the truck, starting a makeshift fire with two grey branches and whatever sun tan lotion Former

FORMER BASEBALL PLAYER SUCKS AT CROWDFUNDING

had left in his bindle. It was more than you'd think. There, the two exchanged stories of their life before the war as Former downed boxes and boxes of indeterminate Thing Testosterone.

"I remember a lot of green, and then the inside of something huge and furry, and then all of it was gone," Boy murmured, opening his heart to his really disappointing father figure.

"Sounds like my ex-wife, heh heh heh," Former laughed. Boy had no idea what he was talking about.

"How far are we now?" Boy asked.

"About 40 miles out, per some calculations I just made up by looking at the placement of the stars or whatever," Former responded. He adjusted his terrycloth cloak, which he'd pieced together from post-apocalyptic gym towels. "Oak Land is big so we'll have to move through it quickly. I know this is too much information for your sheeple brain, but there are … nah it isn't even worth explaining." Former updated his Twitter with the following tweet: ".@boy will never underrtand [sic] our plan. what is this nation coming to?" Nobody read it because Twitter had been inactive for a decade, there was no electricity and because everyone with a computer was dead.

"I know we have to avoid the Raiders if we want to get in…"

"How do you know about that, bro?" Former asked.

"They're the most popular gang in the area. I hear they wear all black and do whatever it takes to get what they want, even if they break the rules."

"The only rule of post-apocalyptia is that there ARE no rules," Former demanded, his eyes welling up with tears. "If I had it all to do over again I would've joined them. I should've been a two-sport star."

"What are sports, Former?" Boy asked.

"Who knows," Former farted dismissively.

Former Baseball Player opened up a fresh box of steroids and dug in, leaving Boy to sit by the coconut-smelling fire in silence. Boy's eyes wandered into the surrounding forests, still grey even though it was nighttime, trying to make out shapes and movement in the ever-growing darkness. For some reason his vision focused on a particular patch of darkness, and in the flicker of a rogue ember he saw a face. There was a man in the forest watching them ... and although he only saw him for a moment, Boy recognized him.

"Former!" Boy whisper-shouted. "Someone's watching us ... and he looks like you!"

"Hurm?" Former responded, his mouth full of something's bile, or whatever steroids are made out of.

Boy tried to find the face again, but it was gone.

"There was someone in the darkness with your face, watching us," boy continued. "Maybe I'm ... maybe I'm just starving to death and seeing things."

FORMER BASEBALL PLAYER SUCKS AT CROWDFUNDING

"No, you weren't seeing things," Former nodded. "It was Other Former Baseball Player. He's been following us for three days."

"OTHER Former Baseball Player?" Boy cried, incredulously.

"My brother. My twin brother. He was never as good as me and can't do anything for himself. Most people who see him just think he's an error. If we ignore him, he'll go away. Most people haven't thought about him in 25 years."

Boy listened intently. He locked eyes with Former, and they shared a heavy-handed, father-son bonding moment.

"Are you hungry?" Former asked.

"Yes sir, ever so much," Boy smiled back.

"Well, here." Former dug through his 30th box of steroids looking for something he could spare, and when he found nothing, he simply gripped the box by the lid and ripped off a section of cardboard. "Eat this," he said. "You'll need your strength for tomorrow's athletics."

Boy took the shard and began gumming it with loud "nom nom nom" noises. "Tomorrow's athletics," he thought to himself. They wouldn't be great, but sabermetrically they'd be what got the team to their end goal.

"Before we go to sleep, I need to tell you something important," Former said quietly. Boy leaned in to listen, still gumming a sad-ass piece of cardboard box. "There may be a moment when Other Former Baseball Player tries to pose as me, replace me. Like at an autograph signing I don't want to go to, or a Celebrity Boxing obligation I don't want to fulfill."

"How can I tell it's him?"

"You gotta get us both on a rooftop and wait for us to struggle, then hold up a gun so we can be like, NO, I'M THE REAL FORMER BASEBALL PLAYER, SHOOT HIM and then the other one goes, NO *I'M* THE REAL ONE, SHOOT HIM. I don't know, ya little a-hole," Former said, joshingly shoving Boy so hard he hit the dirt and slid. "Actually, come t'think of it ... there is one way. "

Former Baseball Player leaned in closer.

"He's got an extremely small penis."

Boy's eyes blinked.

"I mean, it's bigger than MINE, but it's still extremely small. That's literally the only way to tell. We both have such embarrassingly small penises, and his is different."

"I don't ... uh, I don't know what your penis looks like, so it's hard for me to tell who's is who's, and ..."

"All right, stop twisting my arm, here's my penis." Former held up his phone, which somehow still had full charge, possibly because his hands are radioactive conductors, what from all the post-apocalyptic wandering and performance-enhancing substance inhaling. " Also, his phone was just chock full of dick pics. Boy didn't look, because that would be gross. Also, his face was in the dirt.

"Remember my penis," Former reiterated. "Trust me. Most people don't."

FORMER BASEBALL PLAYER SUCKS AT CROWDFUNDING

Boy collected himself and slumped back into a sitting position to finish his cardboard. Former Baseball Player turned back to the truck, then gasped in horror.

"Bro, my shit!" he screamed. The truck was suddenly empty. He had at least two or three boxes of steroids left, he thought. Other Former Baseball Player had struck. "God dammit!"

The next morning, Former Baseball Player and Boy began their long trek from realistically maybe two miles outside of Oak Land to the heart of the city. Set to a mournful, post-pop synthesizer soundtrack, the duo passed several important apocalyptic Oak Land landmarks, such as Heinold's Last And Last Chance Saloon, the Last Unitarian Church on 14th, and the Peralta Hacienda Historical Park, which was basically just six acres of tire fires. After almost a day of walking (because of periodic breaks), Former and Boy reached their destination: the Oak Land Coliseum, where the steampunk ganglords of Neofornia called home. Some say it used to house mediocre sporting contests, but now it's mostly for throwing religiously-nonspecific trespassers to the lions.

Former stopped Boy with a mighty hamfist and pointed up. Boy could see terrifying men standing guard around the top of the stadium walls, wearing the skulls of beasts like the buck, the black bear and Josh Hamilton on their heads as trophy helmets. They were also wearing studded S&M gear, because fashion gets kinda shifty in the future.

"What do we do?" Boy asked.

"My heart says 'tattle on them,' but I'm not sure to whom," Former said. He began to rub his massive rectangular chin, but before he could formulate a plan he was interrupted by a tomahawk flying inches from his head. "Oh crum!" he screamed, and dived behind a grey bush.

"What's going on?" Boy asked. Boy asked a lot of questions like this.

Before Former could answer, a group of Raiders swarmed and circled them. Many of them were wearing eyepatches. Boy looked to Former for help, but Former was already sprinting away down the street. Boy tried to yell out for help, but decided it wasn't worth it, because Jesus Christ, what is wrong with that guy? Without the aid of a giant sociopath, Boy was easily overpowered by the Raiders, who wrapped him up in thick, pirate-style rope and hoisted him onto their shoulders. They marched him toward the Coliseum, and yes, they fumbled him a few times, but they eventually got where they were going.

During the walk, Boy fought off the urge to give in to sadness-starvation and contemplated all the moments that had gotten him here. He'd done pretty well on his own, considering that he was an infant in a grim hellscape who survived not only a world-changing act of violence, but the attack on his native village that'd left everyone but him slaughtered and posted on spikes. As a five year-old he'd put together a small motor scooter through trial and error and had traveled across the country looking for answers, four whole years searching for the truth about his upbringing, before realizing that everything he was looking for was where he started. That's life, isn't it? A lengthy, pointless quest to find answers that are written on a Post-It Note and stuck to your forehead when you're born. He'd found heroism in this awful man, idolizing him for his athletic prowess and excusing him for all his social trespasses, until this moment when it really mattered. This moment when he turned tail and ran, because the only thing important to Former Baseball Player is himself.

    The Raiders tossed Boy into a dark room. He lied there in the dirt for what seemed like days, waiting to wake up from this horrible dream, or to welcome the cold, merciful hand of death, the only angel he'd ever known. He could hear the whispers of other people in the room with him, but he dared not make a sound, for their hands might not be bound, and they might feast upon him. At what he thought were his last moments on Earth, a brilliant light illuminated the room, and Boy looked up to see a sun-lit arch filled with criss-crossed metal bars. Before he could fully focus, the bars were lifted and a room full of sorrowful, abandoned refugees of New America began to herd toward the light. Boy pulled himself up from the dirt, for the last time, he hoped, and followed them.

After a short walk, they found themselves in the infield grass of a baseball diamond. Boy dropped to his knees and tears began to overtake him. Everywhere he looked, he saw the beginning of his life. An expanse of green, an endless spiral of empty seats. He was home. And home was where he would die. He smiled.

Then, a bunch of lions showed up and started eating everybody.

Boy watched as a pack of lions tore the refugees to shreds, laughing in their lion way as they eviscerated every man, woman and child in sight. Boy could hear the Raiders laughing from the stands, and as he turned to look over his shoulder he could see the head Raider, the one they called Dennis, sitting in a throne of bones, cackling into a headset microphone. Behind him was a magnificent circle of bright light, almost as bright as the sun, its colors changing as it swirled. Boy shook his head sadly and looked forward, just in time to duck a swing from a lion's razor-sharp paw. Lifeless, he fell to the ground and heard the lion roar above him. He could feel the lion's saliva dripping down onto his ears. The ferocious animal opened its jaws for the killing blow and pounced, and Boy clenched his eyes tightly, preparing to meet the face of God.

Instead, he met the face of Former Baseball Player.

FORMER BASEBALL PLAYER SUCKS AT CROWDFUNDING

Former Baseball Player, now dressed in a loincloth and a bandolier, charged between Boy and the lion and clasped the beast's mouth with his hands. He held the jaws apart, allowing Boy to scurry to safety.

"I wasn't going to stand by and let you get killed by that fucked-up giraffe!" Former announced.

"I think it's a lion."

"No, lions look more like dogs. Oh I don't know, who cares, who knows things," Former answered, kicking the lion in the throat. He wrapped his arm around the lion's neck, and with a sloppy headlock takeover spun the lion to its death. Triumphantly he stood, wiping lion brains from his protruding chest muscles. Boy looked up in wonder. He was wrong. This truly WAS his father figure, the man he was meant to meet and idolize in this terrible world where only the intangibles and uncertainties make life worth living. He vowed then and there to overthrow Dennis and be the man he knew he could be. Thanks to this magical man, Former Baseball Player.

"Here, let me -- GURKKKK" Former Baseball Player reached out a hand to help Boy up just as the presumably-dead lion jumped up and punched through Former's chest. His heart fell out, and most of his chest bones and guts.

"NOOOOOOOOOOOOO!" screamed Boy. "FORMER BASEBALL PLAYERRRR!!!!"

"What?" answered Former Baseball Player, who was now somehow in the stands behind Dennis.

Dennis was as surprised as anybody, and Former Baseball Player quickly shoved him in the back of his head, knocking him out of his bone throne. Former laughed, making "jerking off and throwing your product" gestures at the Raiders before diving into the spiraling circle of light, disappearing forever.

Boy couldn't believe his eyes. He looked down at the body of what he thought was Former Baseball Player, still lying there gutless in the dirt in front of him. The pieces started to come together in Boy's head. Reluctantly, he lifted the dead man's lion cloth, and after a moment of inspection, his heart sank.

"His is probably much smaller than this," Boy deadpanned. "Well, shit."

And then the lion mauled him.

FORMER BASEBALL PLAYER SUCKS AT CROWDFUNDING

Chapter Eleven

By Casey Malone (@CaseyMalone)

The Year 1865

If you are reading this, then I have been dead and buried for over one hundred and twenty-five years and the truth can finally come out. This letter - this confession - was given to my attorney with strictest instruction, so that when people learn my part in my era's greatest tragedy to befall these United States my children and their children will be gone, safe from the great shame and martyrdom that would surely befall them if this was known today. Even with such assurances my gnarled hands tremble as I attempt to lay bare a truth thought burnt up in that Virginia barn fire so long ago. The truth that I myself am responsible for the downfall of the great emancipator, for the death of President Abraham Lincoln.

I have lived as well a life as I could with this knowledge kept hidden - I have wed, I have sired children, and I have indulged in the wealth that was my rightful inheritance. But any joyful reverie eventually turns quiet, as I am left with my guilt, my nightmare, and my memory of the day I found him, that wretch who I had the ill fate to cross paths with. The creature.

I had moved to Washington D.C. in the spring of 1862. I was so brash then, having left

University to indulge in my father's not insignificant fortune. The War of the Rebellion seemed far and distant from Massachusetts, where I was studying law out of pure inertia and parental demand, and I wanted to be closer to what seemed like excitement. It never occurred to me to fight for the Union, lacking character as I did in those days, but I was drawn to a place where the excitement might also yield the most opportunities for graft, so I headed to our nation's capital.

Not long after arriving I quickly set up my home - a large estate in the Georgetown that was easy enough to keep stocked with alcohol and women. The nearby universities meant no end of hangers-on and cronies to bring me girls in exchange for admittance into my den of celebration. These parties went for days, stopped only when I needed to finally sleep. More than once, in a blind stupid, I fired pistols into the walls of my own home in order to chase guests out to get rest. They always seemed to come back in a few nights when the barrels and bottles were full, so I felt not an ounce of guilt.

Perhaps my guilt seeped into Potomac as I slept. Maybe the shame and self-disgust that should have consumed me instead settled to its basin, taking root in The Nation's River until it had enough, and deciding to take its revenge on me and on the world, spat back out into being him. The Creature.

After years of this, I'd begun to grow tired of the parties and had closed my doors to the masses. My friend William had joined me from Cambridge not long after my arrival, and we'd taken to simply drinking ourselves blind on our own instead of involving the locals. William, sharing my advantage in life and being of similar moral fabric, was the perfect accomplice. We took an open air carriage ride one day to recover from a binge when suddenly, near the river, I saw it. At first, the sun in my eyes, I thought I was mistaken. But leaning forward to get a better look, I was sure. Standing stark nude, alone in the weeds of the river, far from any sign of civilization, was something in the form of a man.

I am still not entirely sure if the beast was human. He was larger than any man I'd ever seen, a full head taller than me and his body was a gnarled mass of fatty muscles. His gut was like that of a great ape, protruding yet taut. His arms were massive as tree trunks, unnaturally huge, as if a demon had infused them with power at some terrible cost. We'd come to see later, after we had cleaned the terrible muck and grime off of him, that his skin was less flesh and more leather. It was unclear if he was covered in wrinkles or cracks.

"Hello there!" William cried, trying to get his attention as we approached. The thing swung its glance towards us, its beady, predator eyes sizing us up. Were I wiser then I would have felt fear. William continued to speak to it.

"Are you in need of aid?" he asked. We'd stopped several feet from it, maintaining a safe distance.

"What's this shit?" it mumbled back, at no one in particular. It seemed to be taking in its surroundings, tilting its head left and right in herky-jerky birdlike motions. This went on for a few moments.

"Are you lost? How did you find yourself here in the reeds, dear boy?" William asked.

"I dunno," it said.

"Do you have a name? Where did you come from?"

"I'm the best."

"The best? Why, the best at what?" I asked it. There was a long pause.

"I'm the best."

"I see." I turned to William. "I've never seen anything like him before."

William adopted a hushed tone, but never took his eyes off of it. "Agreed! He could clearly destroy us with all his terrible might, but he just stands there. His childlike demeanor... it's fascinating."

I nodded in agreement, "I think we've just found all the entertainment we need."

After some gentle coaxing, like luring a stray cat from an alley, we were able to get the thing to come to us. Stumbling out of the weeds we wrapped a horse blanket around him and led him into the carriage. His face remained expressionless the entire time, and throughout the ride back to my estate. Even when William caught glimpse of the thing's genitals, which hanged curiously shriveled, and let out a snicker... the beast remained stoic.

FORMER BASEBALL PLAYER SUCKS AT CROWDFUNDING

Arriving home, William paid the carriage driver to keep quiet what he'd seen while I brought our new project inside. Letting the horse blanket fall to the foyer's floor, he surveyed his new surroundings as he had before. I reached for a carafe of bourbon that I kept in the entry way for guests and poured myself a drink. As the liquid hit my glass he sniffed the air suspiciously.

"Do...do you want a drink?" I gently shook the decanter, but before I knew what was happening, he was upon me, snatching it out of my hand and downing my whiskey in one long gulp. He exhaled proudly and let the container hit the floor, shattering it.

"WOO!" he shouted. He seemed alert for the first time since being found.

William entered and I cautioned him about the broken glass littering my entry way.

"Well, now what?" William said. Excited by liquor, the beast casually flipped an end table, smashing it. He laughed.

"Now, I think, we get him clean."

My servants were summoned to bring the hulking mass up to the washroom where they filled a tub with soap and hot water. William and I watched, smoking, as they lowered him in, grime falling off him in sheets. He fought being prodded and groomed, especially resentful of the poor woman tasked with scraping eons of dirt out from beneath his nails, recoiling each time she approached a new nail.

"Uncool!" he shouted, splashing her with water with his free hand. "I'm the best."

"How old do you think he is?" William turned to me, "He's surely at least twice our age, yet he's fitter than any old man I've seen, and he behaves like a feral child."

"I haven't a clue." The term feral turned over and over in my head. "Do you think... do you think he can be domesticated?"

"How do you mean?"

"Look at him, thrasing about as if he's never seen water! We found him in a damn river. I wonder if we could train him, even bring him into high society without him breaking every damn thing in sight." I puffed my pipe, "You know, make a proper dandy out of him."

"Him?" William laughed. "We'll be lucky if we can get him into a pair of overalls, out in the yard chasing livestock around."

"You think so? Well, how about a wager, then?"

"Ha! Just the thing. The terms?"

"In a few weeks we take him to a high society event. Use whatever influence we can buy to get him among Washington's elite. If it's a success, I win. If it's a disaster, then you're proven right. Either way, we'll likely set him loose in the wild afterward."

"Accepted. We do need some way to refer to him, though."

"True..." The thing currently thrashing about in a tub of water had refused further inquiry about his origins or even his name, during the trip back. I took a long draw from my pipe and thought. He seemed so new to this world, this hulking mass. I thought back and recalled a novel I read as a child, The Modern Prometheus, about a similar story. Thinking "Prometheus" too much of a mouthful, we named him after the author, and from then on only referred to him that way - as Shelley.

We first needed to address the matter of Shelley's nudity, made difficult by his size. There were not clothes in my home, or even in the Capitol, that were built for someone his dimensions. The garments for someone his size, well over six feet, could not contain his gut. The legs of pants for his girth ended just below his knees (though the small inseam was not an issue). In the end I called my personal tailor to measure Shelley, and ordered some bespoke garments for him. They'd take some time to produce, but in the mean we wrapped the horse blanket - unwashed from our first encounter - around his mid-section. He'd occasionally throw it off like an unruly child, but William and I would coax him back into wearing it, if only to silence the female servants' snickering.

Then there was the matter of etiquette. "It hardly will do if we bring him out and he's rude." William pointed out. "The bet was to make him a gentleman, not docile." Irritatingly, William was correct.

We paid one of the servant girls double for to sit with us and try to teach him the proper way to behave around a lady. He mastered standing when she entered the room, but once there he would refuse to sit and leer horribly, grunting and muttering about "cans," for some reason. After days of failure, William and I began using a system - when he did not respond to a cue, we would spray him with a small containers of water. For as much as he hated clothing, Shelley seemed to hate water twice as much.

His aversion to water extended to the drinking of it. Once we had him bowing, standing, and shaking hands at the proper times - we still could not get him to introduce himself in any manner other than declaring he was "the best" or "the greatest" - we moved on to dinner time manners. In all of our lessons we could not get Shelley to eat or drink anything other than brown liquor, which he did greedily.

Barrel after barrel of bourbon whiskey were ordered in the short time we worked with him, but he imbibed in a way that put William and my previous benders to shame. His propensity to shout out bizarre phrases such as "That is my shit!" or "Hell yeah, bro!" before throwing the container to the floor necessitated we serve him from deep wooden bowls rather than glassware. The most astonishing thing was not his consumption of it, but that his demeanor outside of those quick ejaculations was so simple and blank that it was impossible to determine if he was intoxicated or not.

It was during one of our faux-meals to teach him manner that an acquaintance of William's stopped by. He was an actor, having recently finished playing Duke Pescara in *The Apostate* at Ford's Theater. William knew him from his days seducing young actresses, and his friend had been a member of a touring company William and become entangled in.

"John," he said as he brought him into the room, "This...is Shelley."

John's eyes widened as he took in Shelley's frame. Shelley was drinking from his bowl when John entered, and stood up as he had been trained. He did not, though, stop drinking. The two maintained eye contact as Shelley gulped the rest of his bourbon.

"What the devil is this thing?" John asked.

"He's a man!" I said, delighted. "Or at least, we're making him into one."

"His gut, his arms... my god. It's not natural." John spoke in a reverent, fearful tone, "He's as much of an abomination as I've ever seen. Can't you see that?"

"If he has feelings," I said, finding myself surprisingly defensive, "I'm certain you're doing them harm." Shelley did not appear to understand he was being spoken about.

"I'm the best." he uttered.

"Bill," John said, turning to William, "I've known you a long time but I am not sure what you've gotten mixed up in here. That thing is more animal than man, he's unholy."

"Well, that's what we're trying to discover," William seemed to not entirely disagree with John, but was making our case. "We're trying to see if he can be made into a man. We're going to bring him to a gala, a banquet, a-"

"A play!" I declared. I'd grown annoyed with the tone William's friend payed towards Shelley. He might have been a silent, brutish monster, but I had finally found a project and did not appreciate the disrespect. John scoffed.

"He more belongs in a circus! A play indeed." John shook his head, growing more heated than I even expected. "The day you bring this thing into a theater, a place sacred to me, is the day I end its existence." A tense quiet fell over the room after these words fell. The quiet was broken, mercifully, when Shelley let out a deafening belch from the whiskey.

"Right on." Shelley said.

"Okay, John," William was quickly shuttling his friend out of my house, rightly so. "Let's perhaps take this conversation up the road to a tavern and cool down."

They left, but I was still indignant. From that moment, it was decided, we would bring Shelley to a play, to the most exclusive event of the season, and we would use all of our wealth and connections to get him the best seat in the house.

"I don't think he liked you much," I said, turning to Shelley.

"I'm the fucking best." Shelley argued back.

When William returned I told him of the plan. He seemed trepidatious and warned that John's threats weren't idle. He was a man of extreme conviction, even when those convictions weren't in the right. I reassured that there was nothing to worry about - what would he do, stage fight Shelley to death? I tasked William with using his theater connections to discover the most prestigious night at Ford's Theater to bring Shelley to. To our delight, we discovered that the theater owner's brother could not stop bragging that in a week's time, on Good Friday, President Lincoln himself would be in attendance for a production of "Our American Cousin." That had to be it - we expected to gauge the reaction of a few senators and congressmen, but to see how the greatest man in the nation reacted? It was perfect.

We spent the following 6 days in a flurry of preparations. We were able to get Shelley to respond to certain cues and adhere to standards we set. We abandoned the table rules since there was no dinner portion of our evening at the theater, and focused on simple interaction with adults. He would no longer grunt and leer at women when they entered his vision, though this behavior was quizzically replaced with him nodding in approval and muttering, "Nice..." under his breath. He also would shake hands and smile when prompted, though the smile rarely spread to his those bead-like eyes of his. All marked improvements.

The night of the play, William arrived early with Shelley's new custom suit, and we had the servants clean and dress him. He emerged from the house as we waited near the carriage and we were taken aback by the transformation. There was nothing to be done about his blank expression, or his terrifying eyes which darted back and forth, but the muscular frame, freakish as it was, filled out the hand crafted suit well.

"I'd say that if the servants hadn't already seen his significant shortcomings," William said, indelicately, "They might even be taken with him." Hearing him admit this made me feel doubly hopeful for my chances in the wager. I distinctly remember thinking, not knowing what was to come, that it's possible the evening might not end in disaster.

My nerves returned not long after our arrival at the theater, however. Stepping out of the carriage, the very first person to lay eyes on us was William's friend John.

"You bastards," John spat, "How dare you dress that thing as a man and bring him here?"

"John, come now." William pleaded.

"No. No! You've been warned." John was visibly reddened. "Now you'll have to live with the consequences." He stormed off into the night, leaving us outside, a small crowd gathered half to observe the fight, and half to stare at Shelley.

"What a pussy." Shelley said to no one in particular. We had made our entrance.

Inside the theater, Shelley performed beautifully, shaking hands and nodding as if he were listening. He said almost nothing, and William and I did most of the speaking for him. He's from a far off land, a dignitary from foreign soil, we lied. English is not his first language,

FORMER BASEBALL PLAYER SUCKS AT CROWDFUNDING

we'd say, and as Senators and other actual dignitaries would shake his hand gratefully we'd turn our heads behind Shelley's massive back and laugh.

During one such giggle fit, an employee of the theater approached William and whispered something in his ear. Suddenly, he went ashen and turned to me suddenly serious.

"I think we should go."

"Why in God's name would we go? Wait, you're not getting out of the bet that easily, this is going perfectly."

"I concede, Shelley has gone beyond every expectation, you win the bet."

"I'm the best." Shelley said, looking at the both of us. I ignored him and turned back to William.

"What's going on here, we haven't even met the President yet."

"That's just it," William whispered, "I apparently pulled too many strings, and now it appears we're guests of the president's private box."

I began howling with laughter. How could I have dreamed of a more perfect evening? Shelley certainly could maintain this level of decorum for a moment with Mr. Lincoln, but to sit next to him for three entire acts? Who knows what could happen! Shelley's shown so few reactions to the world around him, and here we were at an acclaimed farce. Would his icy silence unnerve the greatest man in the nation, who days prior ended a war? Could we cause such societal discomfort as to get ejected? In my youth and naiveté it felt like a great accomplishment to be impolitely asked to leave by a president or his wife. Any remaining worry from our run in with John earlier had left me.

At my insistence, we moved to the presidential box immediately. The presidential party was late, and William fidgeted nervously, losing his spine now that we were in the thick of it. Shelley sat silently, finding the appropriate middle distance to stare into. I was just getting settled into a comfortable wait when the door opened and in walked an Army Major and his fiancé, making their introductions. They were followed, without any fanfare, by the first lady Mary Todd Lincoln, and the President of the United States Mr. Abraham Lincoln.

I cannot do proper service to my encounter with the man. My mischievous intent fell away almost immediately, and I found myself in William's same panic. We had brought a beast into the room with the president, and now we were trapped here.

"Nice to meet you young men." Mr. Lincoln said to us. I don't rightly remember my response, or William's, the entire evening was such a blur, but I remember the next few moments with utter clarity.

Shelley stood, and approached the president. They were matched for height exactly, two giants, sizing each other up.

"A pleasure to meet you son," Lincoln held out his hand.

FORMER BASEBALL PLAYER SUCKS AT CROWDFUNDING

After an unearthly long pause, Shelley's expression changed from blank to that of recognition. Something deep within him stirred. He opened his mouth to speak, closed it, looked the president up and down one last time and opened it again.

"You're the penny guy." he said, gripping Mr. Lincoln's hand.

Lincoln shook his hand while placing the other on Shelley's enormous shoulder. His kind eyes exuded sympathy - he clearly understood Shelley to be simple. Perhaps his great gift of empathy allowed him to look into Shelley's soul, and see the great emptiness therein, and the great deficit in Shelley's genitals. There's no way to tell what Lincoln saw, but he responded with warmth.

"I tell you, I've met people like you before," the president laughed, "But never this big. It's a pleasure to take in the theater with you, my friend."

I breathed a sigh of relief and Shelley nodded his empty nod, sitting back down. We all settled in and I realized that the evening would work out in my favor. Hours later, deep into act three, as we all know now, that favor changed dramatically for the worse.

The play was coming to a conclusion when, suddenly, the door to the booth opened and William's friend John appeared. Before we could question his appearance, he barricaded the door to the box.

"John, what are you-" William demanded before being cut off.

"Quiet, Bill! I told you! I told you what would happen if you brought that thing here." John reached into his pocket and brandished a pistol. He pointed it towards Shelley.

We all stood immediately, the play still going on behind us. The president put the first lady behind him as John continued to rant about Shelley.

"I don't know where that thing comes from, but it surely is an unholy, unnatural time. Look at him! How did he gain such size? What horrible atrocities did he engage in to give his very presence such an electric air of nightmare? You've brought this thing into my home, Bill, and I am now going to remove it." John cocked the lock on the pistol.

"Come at me bro." Shelley said, taking a step towards John. This was all the threat John needed.

Then it happened. The event I still blame myself. I don't know why he did it, why it was him willing to take the pistol's bullet for Shelley and not the other way around. But with his last act of nobility on this earth, President Abraham Lincoln jumped in front of the pistol and took the wound meant for Shelley.

John, in a panic, disappeared immediately, presumably struck with the enormity of what he had done. Mrs. Lincoln collapsed immediately and as William tried to save her from her fall, I saw that Shelley was

holding the dying president in his arm.
"My friend," Lincoln said weakly, his life leaving his body and staining Shelley's newly tailored suit, "Your simplicity is beauty, and your right to find your happiness in the face of tyrants is what makes American great." Lincoln coughed, "I would take this grave wound for you a hundred times if I could, for you are truly beautiful." These were his last words, as the body of Lincoln went limp and lifeless.

Shelley laid Lincoln's corpse gently on the ground and nodded in agreement. "I'm the best," he said.

Shelley then rose, as large as a mountain, and stepping over the body of our fallen leader and around William and Mrs. Lincoln, he exited the box without a word. Stunned and bloodstained, I chased after him. He was already halfway down the hall out of Ford's Theater.

"Wait, where are you going?" I shouted at him through tears. "Who ARE you? Don't you understand what's happened here you great beast?"

He looked at me. He knew that this was my fault, that he had simply stumbled into our lives and that I was the one who made every decision which led to tonight. Shelley knew that I would be forced to live with the guilt of what I did for the rest of my life. But he didn't say any of that. He simply looked at me and said something as odd as anything else he'd said in the short few months I knew him.

"Party's dead, bro." The thing I'd named but never truly knew closed his eyes and nodded solemnly to himself. "I'm going to go see if I can find some fuckin' trim."

And then he was gone.

The rest of that evening escapes me. William and I were detained by the law for questioning, but they could find no trace of the beast anywhere. No one knows where he went. Some witnesses claimed seeing a hulking giant in an alley arguing with known whores, but no one could confirm that. One witness said they saw the silhouette of a freakish monster against a streetlamp, then there came a great flash and it was gone, inexplicably. With a much greater purpose pressing, the police never followed up.

William and I never spoke again. His friend John was burnt to death in Virginia in a farm when he refused to turn himself in. I returned to law school and tried to forget the entire event, but as this letter in your hands is evidence of anything, it's that I was incapable of doing so. The truth is out now, and perhaps in the afterlife I found rest.

My breaking point, the moment I needed to expel these thoughts to paper in hopes that one day the truth can come out, comes during what I believe to be near the end of my days. As I write this I am man in my seventies, in the year of our lord 1909. Recently, I made a purchase, getting confections for some of my grandchildren. The boy working the pharmacy handed me my change and I saw it in my hand. With its copper gleam I was transported back to that night in April, 1965. A penny. With Lincoln's head. My heart pounded and I grew dizzy as the beast's words to the president hours before he was killed rang through my ears.

"You're the penny guy."

The one question from this mess I take to my grave without answer. So I beg you, reader, illuminate the truth, share this story, so we that it might be discovered. How. How in the hell did he know?

DAN RYCKERT AND FRIENDS

FORMER BASEBALL PLAYER SUCKS AT CROWDFUNDING

Chapter Twelve

By Dan Ryckert

The Year 2033

As he prayed that his journey was near its end, Former Baseball Player was hurled from the portal onto the grass below. Looking up, he didn't know whether to expect dinosaurs, a futuristic cityscape, or horse-drawn carriages. At this point, anything was possible. Shielding his eyes from the afternoon sun, he saw the clear outline of the Washington Monument. After laughing for several minutes thanks to the structure's resemblance to an erection, he was suddenly reminded that it in no way reflected the proportions of his own flaccid, microscopic phallus.

His spirits were lifted when he recalled seeing the same monument during a field trip in third grade, which was coincidentally his current reading level. For the first time in his chaotic journey, he immediately knew where he was. Now, it was only a matter of learning the time. Many tourists posed for pictures in front of the Washington Monument, and he approached a lone woman.

"Hey lady when is this?" he asked.

Unnerved by the monstrous, dirty man approaching her, the woman hopped on a nearby floating scooter and began to escape.

"Hey don't be scared space lady I just wanna know the year!" he yelled. "I'm tired of dudes in funny wigs and stupid hats and robots and shit, and you're pretty."

"It's 2033, you idiot!" she yelled as she rushed away on the futuristic device.

"Whoa..." Former Baseball Player said to himself as he attempted to do the math between 2013 and 2033. "I gotta be like 100 or something now."

Instead of embarking on the more-interesting quest to find his future self (who would actually be 70), his thoughts immediately turned to Dan Ryckert. Simply getting money from the successful writer was no longer enough for the former athlete. He recalled seeing the film *Back to the Future* at some point, and for some reason decided that killing the author would put an end to his time-traveling ordeal.

Being decades in the future, Former Baseball Player had no idea where Ryckert lived or if he was even still alive.

"Hey dude!" FBP yelled as he approached a man taking a picture of the National Mall's

FORMER BASEBALL PLAYER SUCKS AT CROWDFUNDING

reflecting pool. "Do you know who Dan Ryckert is?"

"You kiddin'?" asked the man. "Everyone knows who Dan Ryckert is. He's the eccentric billionaire playboy author that's on the cover of every magazine out there right now!"

Former Baseball Player was too dumb to be surprised about multiple print magazines still existing in 2033 (outside of *Game Informer*, the world's #1 video game magazine), and he immediately became jealous of Ryckert's billionaire status.

"He made *billions* off of me?" FBP said.

"Offa you? Hell boy, I don't even know who you are. Naw, he made it playing the stock market!"

Former Baseball Player was unaware that in 2011, Dan Ryckert bought three hundred dollars of Arby's stock purely on the basis of their delicious food. The author never bothered to do any research on how the stock market works or how to make a good investment, but he really liked Arby's and wanted to own stock in them. Despite the fact that the fast food chain no longer offered that awesome "5 for $5" deal that let you get a ton of awesome shit for super cheap, their business had skyrocketed for the past two decades. Even without that sweet deal, there was no denying that Arby's Melts, curly fries, mozzarella sticks, and potato wedges were still the best thing, and the American population's craving for them grew and grew until Arby's toppled McDonald's as the most profitable fast food chain in the world. Ryckert's blind, uneducated investment had grown from $300 to untold billions, and his reputation as a charismatic internet personality grew exponentially throughout the years.

"Yep, he's probably the most famous guy in the country right now!" the tourist said. "Hell, he's been all over the news lately since he's competing in the Capitol Carnage tournament tomorrow!"

"What's Capitol Carnage?" FBP asked.

"How stupid are ya, boy? It's been the national sport for the last five years! This crazy dude named Kulipso holds a car combat tournament each year, and grants one wish for the winner! I don't know what kinda witchcraft that dude is usin', but he always makes good on his promise!"

With that, Former Baseball Player knew what needed to be done. He'd enter the tournament, humiliate and kill Ryckert, and then receive the bonus of any wish he could possibly fathom. In an instant, everything that was wrong with his life could be fixed. Without saying another word to the helpful tourist,

FORMER BASEBALL PLAYER SUCKS AT CROWDFUNDING

Former Baseball Player sprinted towards the signup kiosks located in front of the U.S. Capitol Building.

As he excitedly scrawled his name on the signup sheet with the handwriting finesse of a raccoon, he was informed that he'd need a vehicle to participate. Upon hearing this news, he glanced around and noticed the woman on the hover scooter from before. She briefly stepped off to snap a picture of the Capitol, and Former Baseball Player pushed her into a fountain and stole the scooter from her.

"You limp-dicked asshole!" the woman yelled at Former Baseball Player as he laughed and scooted away.

There was only one thing he had left to do to prepare for the big day tomorrow. He spent the entire night scooting around the futuristic Washington D.C., offering a wide variety of humiliating sexual favors to anyone with access to steroids. Never pausing to sleep, the former athlete spent the wee hours of the morning sitting in a pile of syringes, injecting dose after dose of the future's unbelievably potent anabolic steroids into his pockmarked, leathery buttcheeks. He would be ready, and Ryckert had no idea what was about to hit him.

"Ladies and gentlemen of the United States," the wispy, dark-suited man known as Kulipso said from behind a podium. "Welcome...to Capitol Carnage!"

Thousands of fans flooded the perimeter of the National Mall on the fifth annual Capitol Carnage Day, many holding signs and chanting for its undisputed star, Dan Ryckert.

"I hear your voices loud and clear, citizens." Kulipso continued. "And I'm here to listen to you, the fans. To kick off this tournament, we'll have a few words from the undefeated champion of the past four Capitol Carnage tournaments...Dan Ryckert!"

A roar emanated from the crowd, its volume unprecedented in the history of the tournament. It only got louder as the author of the successful *Air Force Gator* series took to the stage, adorned with his four ornate championship belts, a crown made of pure diamond, and his newly-trademarked sequined robe.

"I welcome you once again, my followers!" Ryckert said. "Many of you have been with me since my meager beginnings. Your purchases of the *Air Force Gator* books financed thousands of delicious and affordable Bud Light for me in my younger days, and you've continued to support me into my glorious middle age. You supported

FORMER BASEBALL PLAYER SUCKS AT CROWDFUNDING

me during my tumultuous divorces with Kate Beckinsale, Famke Janssen, Trish Stratus, and that super hot bartender lady from the Vegas Lounge in Minneapolis. You've also financed my tickets for numerous pro wrestling events over the years, and I'm ready to return the favor this year. When I win my fifth consecutive Capitol Carnage tournament, I will be using the prize money to take every single one of you to WrestleMania 50 at the OmegaDome in my hometown of Neo-Minneapolis!"

A deafening "Thank You Ry-ckert (clap clap, clap clap clap)" chant could be heard from every person in attendance. If there were any previous doubt who the crowd favorite was, it was extinguished with this display of philanthropy.

The chant continued for ten minutes as Ryckert flexed and waved, but murmurs began to come from the crowd near the podium. *Air Force Gator*'s trailblazing author glanced down at the commotion, and saw the crowd part to reveal something he never thought he'd see again.

Standing over twelve feet tall, an even-more monstrous version of Former Baseball Player broke through the crowd and stared Ryckert down. His head was somehow way fatter than before, and his stupid cartoon arms were at least five times their previous size. When Ryckert last saw FBP, he was a sad, old, tiny-penised has-been. Now, he was a hulking, terrifying, small-penised has-been.

"*Former Baseball Player?!*" Ryckert said in shock.

"Fuck yeah it is," FBP replied. "And I'm finally gonna beat the shit out of you. You're dead today, you fucking leech."

Flustered, Ryckert still needed to keep up his confident persona.

"It's...it's certainly a surprise to see you, Former Baseball Player. I haven't seen your dumb head in twenty years."

"I was busy doing a bunch of stupid crap in the past, but I'm ready to give you what you deserve. I'll see you in the finals, you fucking nerd."

"Do you *see* these?" Ryckert said as he held his belts above his head. "You don't stand a chance. Besides, do you even have a vehicle fit for this tournament?"

"I got one of these space scooters."

"Oh man," Ryckert laughed. "Good luck, dipshit. I'm sure that'll hold up just great against this bad boy."

Ryckert pointed towards the combat area, where his trusty vehicle sat on display. When he first came into riches, Ryckert's first purchase was the sweet monster truck that Steve Austin

FORMER BASEBALL PLAYER SUCKS AT CROWDFUNDING

used to smash The Rock's car before WrestleMania XV. It sat in pristine condition, still adorned with a bunch of skulls and 3:16 decals. The only thing Ryckert had changed about the classic automobile was the addition of numerous rocket launchers and automatic weaponry.

Kulipso approached the podium once again.

"Gentlemen, gentlemen," Kulipso said. "Let's save this anger for Capitol Carnage! Funnel your hatred into this grand event, and we'll see who the true victor is!"

"Fine," Ryckert said as he spit towards FBP. "Suck my dick, Former Baseball Player."

"Let the games begin!" Kulipso said as the tournament officially started.

Throughout the afternoon, Ryckert figuratively and literally crushed his opponents under the weight of his heavily-armored monster truck. Every totalled police car, hearse, ice cream truck, and taxi brought the author closer and closer to his rightful place in the tournament's final.

On the other end of the bracket, Former Baseball Player made waves by breaking from Capitol Carnage tradition. After struggling to keep his bulging legs balanced on the scooter during the first round, the idiotic athlete opted to sprint around the National Mall while using his newly found super-strength to burn through the competition. The crowd erupted each time Former Baseball Player lifted an automobile over his head and cracked it in half by bringing it down over his knee. Many drivers attempted to flee their automobiles when they saw Former Baseball Player approach, but the athlete's unnatural speed couldn't be matched. He grabbed competitor after competitor and took them to their grave by headbutting them to death or repeatedly smashing their faces into the Vietnam Memorial wall. His rage fueled a historic performance in the tournament, only subsiding occasionally when he'd catch a glimpse of the Washington Monument and be reminded of his Lilliputian penis.

Both Ryckert and Former Baseball Player continued their thrilling performances throughout the afternoon and evening, and the National Mall was littered with flaming metal and the corpses of fallen combatants by sundown. Above the Mall was a massive bracket that displayed the very thing that the crowd wanted more than ever in the finals. Dan Ryckert would be taking on Former Baseball Player in a fight to the death.

FORMER BASEBALL PLAYER SUCKS AT CROWDFUNDING

"Capitol Carnage fans, your attention please!" Kulipso shouted into the podium's microphone in an attempt to settle the raucous crowd. "The time has come! Each and every one of you is about to witness the greatest main event in the history of this great sport. The defending champion Dan Ryckert will be facing his greatest threat to date. This new monstrosity seemingly cannot be stopped! Will your hero be able to retain his title for the fifth consecutive year against this new, mysterious challenger?"

Dueling chants rang out from the crowd, with one half yelling "Let's go Ry-ckert!" followed by the other half responding "F-B-P!" This continued for several minutes as tension mounted among the audience.

Without warning, the massive lights that covered the Mall shut down. An explosion of flames and sparks came from the direction of the Washington Monument, and Dan Ryckert's skull-covered monster truck ramped through the deafening pyrotechnics. The crowd roared for minutes as Ryckert tore through the grass of the Mall to the guitar solo of "Free Bird," frequently ramping off his fallen foes' vehicles and landing in time with additional pyro. He eventually finished his grandstanding and drove the awesome vehicle to the designated starting area. Staring towards the entrance near the

Monument, Ryckert revved his engine in anticipation of his opponent's arrival.

In a stunningly bad choice of entrance music, the hulking figure of Former Baseball Player emerged on his hover scooter to the tune of Burl Ives' "Froggy Went A-Courtin'." Drooling, he scooted up to his starting position and stared down Ryckert through the windshield of the monster truck.

"It's about to be over, asshole," Former Baseball Player yelled across the field.

"Good luck with that, you Crayola-dicked dumbass," Ryckert replied as he continued to rev his motor.

A countdown timer above the National Mall counted down from 10 as the mortal enemies stared each other down from across the field. As it read zero, Kulipso fired a pistol into the air and Ryckert immediately sped towards Former Baseball Player and his dumb scooter thing.

The crowd was silent as Ryckert appeared ready to turn Former Baseball Player into a red stain on the grass. Just before impact, FBP lowered his massive shoulder towards the monster truck. The athlete stayed firmly in place as Ryckert's monster truck crashed into his body. Reeled backwards, the truck's front bumper dramatically crushed inward. A roar

FORMER BASEBALL PLAYER SUCKS AT CROWDFUNDING

escaped the crowd as Ryckert scrambled to create more distance between himself and his surprisingly capable foe.

"I guess that's kind of impressive," Ryckert said through the monster truck's PA system. "Well fuck you dude, let's see how you deal with this."

The author flipped a switch on his dashboard, and two homing missiles burst from the monster truck. Another hush swept over the crowd as they again anticipated a grisly murder. Former Baseball Player caught both missiles in mid-air, and ate the front half of one with a gigantic bite. Ryckert stared on in horror as FBP wound up his arm and tossed the second missile back at its owner. It struck Ryckert's monster truck in its severely damaged grill, and the explosion caused the entire vehicle to go up in flames.

"F-B-P! F-B-P!" the crowd chanted, unanimously turning their support to this spectacular newcomer. He looked around with a dopey grin and waved at his new fans.

From the wreckage of the Stone Cold Steve Austin monster truck, a coughing and soot-covered Dan Ryckert emerged. With his ornate sequined robe in tatters, he began to run away from Former Baseball Player.

Kulipso approached the microphone.

"What is this?" he asked the crowd. "Has our former champion met his match? Surely he knows that submission is not an option in Capitol Carnage. The only way to lose is by death!"

Former Baseball Player knew that his chance was now. He folded up his dumb little space scooter thing into one long piece of metal. He took several steps before hurling the object skyward like he had thrown so many javelins in high school track. As it soared through the Washington, D.C. sky, Ryckert had a moment to turn and see it heading in his direction.

Ryckert had a brief chance to change course and dodge the incoming projectile, but his utterly destroyed wardrobe thwarted him. With his underpants torn apart by the explosion, Dan Ryckert's gargantuan penis unfolded from his trousers and dropped between his legs. As he attempted to dive out of the way of the scooter, his legs became entangled with his phallus that was several feet long while flaccid. He fell to the ground hard, greeted by a facefull of dirt and debris.

Before Ryckert could free his legs from his python-like member, Former Baseball Player's weaponized scooter crashed down through the author's chest. A wet cough of blood erupted

FORMER BASEBALL PLAYER SUCKS AT CROWDFUNDING

from Ryckert's mouth as the athlete stalked over to his prey.

Former Baseball Player looked down at the dying Ryckert as the crowd cheered their new hero. A smile crept across his face as he realized that everything was about to be over. His greatest nemesis was dying in front of his very eyes, a crowd of red-blooded Americans was chanting his name, and he'd be granted any wish his tiny brain could think of.

Ryckert accepted his fate and stopped trying to pull the scooter out of his chest. Looking up at Former Baseball Player, he uttered his last words.

"Hey dipshit..." Ryckert said. "This may be the end for me, but never forget that you're a failure. You're a huge celebrity and you could barely raise a few hundred dollars for that dumb thing you wanted. I'm an idiot that writes about video games and I raised thousands of dollars for nothing. All that matters is that I got that money and got to go to WrestleMania XXX thanks to it. That's the only war that mattered to me. You can take this victory, you idiot. I lived a great life, and you'll always be a fat-headed piece of shit with the world's tiniest dick. See you in Hell, Former Baseball Player."

The light left Ryckert's eyes as his lifeless head fell back against the heap of twisted metal his body laid on.

Not knowing what else to do, Former Baseball Player turned towards the crowd and raised his ham-like fists into the air. Fireworks erupted from every corner of the National Mall as Kulipso approached the new champion.

"Congratulations, Former Baseball Player!" the host said as he presented the athlete with a ludicrously oversized trophy. "You've done what many said could never be accomplished. Whether it was you or his own penis that was his ultimate undoing, the legendary Dan Ryckert is dead and gone. All hail the new champion of Capitol Carnage!"

Some sweet guitar riffs blared from the Mall's many speakers as pyro continued to explode over the roaring crowd. Former Baseball Player had never smiled so much in his life. His eyes scanned over the adoring crowd as they continued chanting his name.

"There's just one more order of business," Kulipso said as the crowd grew quiet in an effort to hear. "It's time for your wish."

"I can have anything? Anything in the world?" Former Baseball Player asked.

"Absolutely anything. No reward is beyond my ability. My powers are great, and I can grant

FORMER BASEBALL PLAYER SUCKS AT CROWDFUNDING

you anything in the world that you wish for. Riches beyond your wildest imagination, the most beautiful women in the world, the power of flight...anything. If you feel burdened by some aspect of your being, let me know and it will be forever gone."

Former Baseball Player couldn't believe that he had ignored this aspect of the tournament all day. His mind was so preoccupied with killing Ryckert, he neglected to think of what was possible with any wish he desired. It was finally time to right a wrong that had cursed him for decades. The athlete slowly glanced down towards his legs as he prepared to wish for what he had desired for so long.

"Kulipso, I know what I want."

"Your wish is my command," Kulipso said.

Former Baseball Player inhaled deeply as he felt his heart beat faster.

"Do you remember the commercials for those bouncy moon boot things back in the 80s?"

Kulipso stared blankly at the athlete.

"No. No I don't."

"They were fucking rad, but they were always sold out when I wanted to get them. A bunch of idiot kids got hurt because of them, so they took them off the shelves before I could get a pair. That's my wish. I want a pair of those cool moon boot bouncy shoes."

"But Former Baseball Player," Kulipso stammered in disbelief. "I'm offering you any wish you could ever think of. A discontinued and frankly dangerous-sounding toy should be very low on a list of possible wishes."

"You said anything! Give me those moon boots, suit man!"

"I...alright, then. Your wish is my command?" Kulipso said as he waved his arms around in dramatic fashion. A cloud of smoke appeared around Former Baseball Player. When it cleared, the athlete's feet were snugly inside two rubbery, neon green boots with springs on the bottom.

"FUCKING SWEET!" Former Baseball Player said as he began bouncing up and down.

As Former Baseball Player bounced off the field and into the Washington night, no element of his time traveling adventures stuck in his mind. His tiny brain had no frame of reference for the stunning sights he had seen, no way to comprehend how many of his idiotic actions had dramatically changed the course of history. All that mattered was that Dan Ryckert was dead and a pair of cool moon boots were on his feet.

Former Baseball Player hopped and hopped until he couldn't hop any more, and eventually collapsed into a pile of hay in the farmlands of Virginia. Nothing in the world could wipe the smile from his face as he drifted off into the most peaceful sleep he had ever experienced in his long, dumb life.

THE END

Acknowledgements

Putting this book together was kind of a pain in the ass, but it was worth it if it means something this fucking stupid will be an actual thing that someone can buy.

Obviously, I want to thank the hilarious contributors to this book. In my original crowdfunding page, I said something about how I'd do the bare minimum required to make something that was technically a book. Instead of just typing total nonsense for a while in an effort to meet that non-goal, I figured it'd be more fun to do something silly with it. I couldn't have done it without the ten awesome contributors to this book.

Many, many thanks to Justin McElroy, Max Scoville, Mitch Dyer, Mikey Neumann, Tim Ryder, Jason Berger, Dave Hinkle, Dave Rudden, Brandon Stroud, and Casey Malone. I owe you all beer.

Thanks to artist Mike Nevins for another awesome cover. Your art is way too good for my shitty-ass books.

Also, a huge thank you to anyone who contributed to the aforementioned crowdfunding campaign that is in no way related to this book. You guys are awesome.

I'm going to WrestleMania!!!

Printed in Great Britain
by Amazon.co.uk, Ltd.,
Marston Gate.